Jill Miller   *Photo by Mary and Mac Macarthur*

Happy as a Dead Cat is Jill Miller's first novel, and it arises from the author's experience of seeing life from a working class angle, and being brought up in a working-class culture, where oppression is none too subtle, and painfully below the belt.

'I take great pride in my ancestors,' she writes, 'who in coming from the four corners of the world, and colourful, lived without prejudice, and loved without reservation, a gift handed to me at birth.'

Jill sees her feminism as part of the fight to liberate all peoples.

Multinational and multicultural, amongst her forbears she boasts Sir Alfred Gilbert, and her Auntie Cherry. She draws from very rich sources.

JILL MILLER

Happy as a Dead Cat

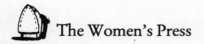 The Women's Press

For John, my friend, lover, and confidant;
Kimberley and Charlotte, our magnificent
daughters; and Annette Mole, who helped to make
this book possible.

For everyone who has ever stood beside me, and
pointed in the right direction.

Thank you Ada Wheeler for the title.

First published in Great Britain by
The Women's Press Limited 1983
A member of the Namara Group
124 Shoreditch High Street, London E1 6JE
Reprinted 1984

First published in the United States by
The Women's Press Limited 1984
Suite 1300
360 Park Avenue South
New York NY 10010

Copyright © Jill Miller 1983

British Library Cataloguing in Publication Data

Miller, Jill
    Happy as a dead cat.
    I. Title
    823'.914[F]   PR6063.I/

    ISBN 0-7043-3898-X

Typeset by MC Typeset, Chatham, Kent
Printed in Great Britain by Nene Litho
and bound by Woolnough Bookbinding,
both of Wellingborough, Northants

One

If shitface asks me what I do with the housekeeping money once more, I'll carve him up with the pissing bread knife. (I happened to be washing up at the time. Had I been hanging clothes on the line I dare say I would have thought of strangling the bleeder.)

'Awful language,' I catch myself saying out loud, and for someone who never swears – well it isn't ladylike, is it?

I can't quite believe it, thirty-seven years of age, and sexism has only just reared its ugly head, or should I say the realisation has only just hit me (and square between the eyes). I say ugly, because since the information has begun to filter through my nappy-clad head, there've been ugly scenes in my/his house.

Oppressed! Of course I'd heard the word before, but I thought it only applied to black people.

'Move those bloody toys,' I shout to a confused two-year-old, 'if I fall over them and break my neck, where will you be then? Your father can't boil a bloody egg without step-by-step instructions.'

I look back at him from across the room. Poor

little sod, what a pig I am, his bottom lip is trembling. I am not falling for it, toss my head and carry on dusting. In two years' time the little crow will be drawing pictures of me, and I'll be wearing a pinafore in every one of them, I just bet.

The duster goes limp as I drift off again.

I wonder if he's sexist already. God what a thought! I wonder if I'm oppressive towards the kids because that's the only area in which I can wield power? It wasn't a question to myself really, more a statement of fact.

Jesus! Valerie! What hope is there for her, am I too late?

She's ten, and already dancing to their tune! She won't wear the school jumper that I bought her last week, wrong shape was the excuse. Could have put her down easily by saying that she was the wrong shape and not the jumper (I left the room just in time). Suppose it's adultist to force her to wear it, never mind – he says I shrink everything – it will fit one of the others after one wash (must suggest that he washes his own woollies).

I even feel powerless around the kids. Back to the dusting.

If I didn't live with him, I wouldn't be bloody well dusting. I stop in my tracks. What could I be doing?

Daydreaming again. Even if I had a job, without him and his critical eye there would be more time to play with the kids.

What day is it? They're all the same, no change in my routine at all. It's Wednesday, my heart sinks, darts tonight for him. He'll fall in around midnight. I'll be in bed pretending to be asleep, he will clatter

2

around the bedroom, dropping his clothes every-where (leaving them for me to pick up in the morning). If that doesn't stir me, he will climb all over me getting into bed, only waiting seconds before the groping starts.

'Have you remembered your pill?' he will tenderly slur. If I'm lucky Rosie will wake up for a feed (if she doesn't I'll kick the ruddy cot).

It isn't lovemaking he wants when he's drunk, it's a quick screw: there again he might even move the sucking child on to the other breast to get there, he's done that before now. Even my body isn't my own (here's food for thought, if our marriage survives the test of time, we will even be buried together, I'll have him chasing me for eternity, cock erect and grabbing at my knickers). At this point I cry, my two-year-old doesn't understand why. My breast is beginning to leak, my milk is coming in, the baby will stir at any time now, and I haven't managed to get it together to preoccupy Thomas. Shit, I'll have two of them kneading at my breasts at this feed.

I may as well just fling myself on the floor in front of my family, and shout, 'Here I am, take whatever bit you want!' I wonder how much would be left.

I catch sight of myself in the hall mirror as I go to lift Rosie from her pram. Not a pretty sight, I think. I give myself a pseudo-smile. Nice teeth though, I count myself lucky I managed to hang on to all of them at each birth, but have two legs that resemble grape vines hanging from road maps.

I never did feel good about my legs, but I don't need any confirmations about their appearance from him (ouch! Rosie's little teeth send electric shocks all over me).

I'm good enough to give birth to his bloody kids, I go on, but not good enough to be seen out with him.

He spends a lot of time in the office lately, why isn't he out on site? Wonder if it's Karen (stupid one-fingered typist qualified for the job by anatomy alone).

I'm starting to cry again, Thomas is casually wiping my tears from his ears, not daring to stop sucking.

Why did I so willingly become a drudge?

I reach over to the window-sill, for a pencil and scrap of paper.

I'm going to make a bloody list of everything I spend my housekeeping money on (*my* house-keeping money, that's a laugh).

Right now, let's see . . . move your head, Thomas. Rosie has fallen asleep. I gently move her and put Thomas on the other breast, definitely not his favourite.

Right, here we go:
£26.25 family allowance
£25 from God (gitface)
£51.25 in all
Coal, one bag one week, two the next at £4.60 per bag, that's (thinks, thinks) £6.90 per week.
£6.90 coal
£2.50 gas meter
£5.00 school dinners
£2.50 washing machine (I treated myself, he had to sign, I pay)
£5.00 catalogue (Xmas presents, it's now March)
£3.00 I put by for clothes for seven people

£2.00 lunch money for Valerie (gone off school dinners)

£3.00 soap, soap powder, toothpaste, washing-up liq, polish, etc etc

£1.00 Xmas hamper (next Xmas)

which leaves a grand total of £20.35 for food, cigarettes (I know I shouldn't, but I do), sweets, papers, and anything over, whoopee, is mine.

Not forgetting sanitary wear, that I will require, until change of life or hysterectomy.

He pays electricity bill, bank loan for house improvements, car insurance, tax, petrol, etc and telephone.

I do damn well. I can't believe that I actually manage when it's all written down like this, but I do. Oh I'd forgotten, if ever I want to go out anywhere, pictures with a friend for example, I scrape that out too. Christ, how many women actually put up with this. I could tear my hair out with anger and frustration, and at the same time I wonder if I could have got it wrong, since the man doesn't seem to have a clue.

'Right, get off me Thomas, that's enough.' Pull down bra, straighten milk-stained jumper. I'll stick this on the television screen. He can't miss it there. Must go shopping.

From now until Friday I have £2.50 for three meals. A quick glance through economy cook book (present from him) for ideas.

I settle for mince, walk a mile to get it for 48p per pound. Trouble with this stuff, I think, squelching it through plastic bag, is that it smells like dog food when it's being cooked. Never mind, if I can organise myself early enough I can open all the windows, use the fresh air spray (which incidentally doesn't smell a lot better than the mince – cheap brand) and sling in the Oxos before he gets in – or the kids for that matter, with their disparaging remarks and turned up noses.

I've just realised (yet another enlightenment) there isn't a meal that I cook, that someone, if not all, doesn't moan, whine or complain about. I usually manage to eat my bit, for all it will pass the lump of resentment in my throat, pushing it between gritted teeth and polite smiles.

How I hate my life, or maybe just the quality of it.

Oh Lord, is it 3.30 already, where did the day go? Did I fall asleep and miss any of it? No such luck.

With Rosie hanging on my breast again (and soul, it feels) I frantically open windows, chasing out the zoo-like smell of the dinner. Oh to sit down to someone else's cooking. When is my wedding anniversary? Come to think of it, shitface gave me a wonderful surprise last year. Surprise was I had to cook it myself.

'Bargain,' he said, thrusting it into my expectant hands (pecking my cheek as he passed, with muttered thanks for eleven years of my life, four kids etc.) then stepping into the bath I had run for myself in the hope of being taken out that evening. 'Now where,' he continued, 'would you get sirloin steak like that for £1 a pound?'

From the back of a bloody lorry, I said to myself.

I burnt his piece, but of course slopped it on to my plate. It was as tough as old boots, but I didn't complain. The wine was pretty ghastly too. That was an offer from the same lorry no doubt.

I managed to smile twice over that dinner; that was the only excuse he had for chasing me up the stairs for an early night. I suppose, if I'm honest, Rosie was the best thing I ever had for an anniversary.

I really hate the pill, continual morning sickness, I'll just have to think of an alternative.

Valerie was a Durex birth, Hazel was a missed pill, Wendy and Thomas were dislodged coils, and Rosie was a Dutch cap. Not a bad record in contraception, me.

He really is a pig. I brought up the subject of vasectomy once. He was raging, said it would make him feel less of a man, tried hard to persuade me to be sterilised after Rosie. Between him and my (male) GP, I was very nearly driven to a nervous breakdown.

'What about me feeling less of a woman?' I asked, to which both replied, while one sneered (not sure which one, either), 'Less of a woman with five children?' Christ will I ever win?

Even though I felt that my back was against the wall, I hung in there, refusing. Rather feel ill on the pill until I've worked something out (keep you thinking, don't they, bloody men).

I dreamed one night I'd cut twenty penises off, and fed them to a pack of wild dogs. He wanted to know why I woke that morning with a grin on my face. Never did tell him. Had an idea I'd live longer if I didn't.

That's the front door slamming. 'Hello Mum, had a good day?' I say to myself, as three small girls (varying in sizes actually) file past me in turn, 'Grunt, grunt, grunt'. Well, at least it's some sort of acknowledgement.

Three school bags now lie in the middle of the kitchen, three coats in disorderly pile at bottom of stairs, and within five minutes one television, one radio and one cassette are blasting three equally awful sounds all over the house. Oh God, I reach out and close windows – neighbours are always complaining. Mince now smells fit for human consumption.

'There's a rabbit in the garden that hasn't seen food for two days,' I yell up the stairs. 'And come down at once and hang these coats up. And take your bags into your rooms!'

All three statements are completely ignored.

I wonder, if I cut my wrists, slumped in a chair bleeding over the furniture, how many of them would notice before I was dead.

Knowing my luck, I would probably survive with a permanent blood disorder from a dirty razor-blade, or something equally horrible.

'Rosie, you're just going to have to cry, I cannot spread myself around any further than I'm doing already.' Quick stir of unsavoury mince. As I step back from the cooker, Thomas yells. I've just crushed his latest matchbox car. Haven't got time to console you, potatoes need to be drained. Shit, where's that dummy (life-saver).

'There, there, son, your wonderful Daddy will be home soon.' (Unless he is working late, with Karen. That thought always creeps in, the crab.)

Damn, no butter or marge for the mashed

8

potatoes. Well improvise, woman. Slop in a cupful of milk. Yuk, I've oversalted them again.

Teatime is the only part of the day when all of us sit down together. And what a misery that is. I wonder why we bother, it almost always ends up in a blood-bath. Our table is continually like a battlefield, with him complaining at all of them for their lousy manners, trying to encourage Thomas to eat his tea, 'whatever it is'. After five minutes, and clouting at least two of them, one will leave the room hastily, slamming a bedroom door to such an extent that the whole of the house shakes with the vibration. My God, it's bad now, am I dreading puberty!

Another meal over. No 'thank yous', plates left on table, floor like a chicken coop. Seems easier to clear the lot and do dishes myself than waste the next hour-and-half trying to encourage one of them to give me a hand. Full of resentment, I just carry on.

He relaxes and reads paper. 'I've been working all day,' he never fails to remind me. And what the hell does he think I've been doing?

I manage to look over his shoulder at my horo-scope for the day. 'An old flame will come back into your life and sweep you off your feet.' My heart sinks and I heave a great sigh. Who would recognise me eleven years and five kids on?

Back to the dishes Cinders. The reality is that there is no prince or knight in shining white armour ever likely to whisk me off on a black or white charger.

I read somewhere once that the only way to let a

9

man know what you do during the day is not to do it. I smile, knowing that it couldn't apply to me with two demanding babies in the house.

Now where the devil is he going tonight? He's running a bath again. Of course what I should have done is downed tools, locked the bathroom door, and stepped into it myself. But I didn't. I break two plates and seethe instead.

'Where are you off to?' I ask lightly, as he trims his moustache over the dishes.

'Doubles knockout,' he answers, not even looking in my direction.

'You didn't mention it this morning.' I try my best not to sound disgruntled, and am spitting chips at his reply.

He stands and stares at me, a real sarcastic expression on his face. 'I'll be going to the toilet in five minutes, and I'll be wearing my blue sweatshirt out tonight. Is that good enough for you?' If he hadn't made a move towards the toilet, the wet dishcloth would have gone right in his gob.

I cling on to the sink in despair until the metal edge cuts into the palms of my hands. I count to ten (well forty-five actually).

'What about me going out for an evening?' I screw up my face in anticipation.

'Go out any time you like,' he shouts back, 'as long as you get a baby-sitter.'

The hairs on my arms stand to attention, but I am not about to back off.

'And what's wrong with you baby-sitting?' I say, adding for good measure 'They *are* your kids too, you know.' There is a deathly silence for a minute or two. I clench my fists tightly.

His voice is slightly softer, but irritated.

'Come on now, after working all day, you don't expect me to come home and start again, do you? A man needs his recreation.'

'What about a woman?' I am quick to answer, to which he pulls the chain.

I start to think about the few times I have been out in the past. I had to make sure the kids and he were fed, I bathed the kids and got them all ready for bed, made sure the house was tidy and everything organised for the next day, and expressed milk for Rosie. By the time I left the house to call for my neighbour I was knackered and ready for bed myself. Carol wasn't at all amused when I fell asleep halfway into the feature film, and even less happy when the usherette poked her to stop me snoring, as the people in front couldn't hear the film.

The look on his face when he comes out of the toilet is enough to convince me that I've been nagging again. I fall into the usual trap of getting jumpy around him, anything to get a pleasant look my way.

'Apple tart in the fridge, love.' (Under my breath, 'Been there a fortnight, might choke or poison you with a bit of luck.')

Ooh, lovely to take the weight off my feet for five minutes in the living room. Can't have had my eyes closed for more than seconds.

'Mum, where's my cookery things for tomorrow?' and 'Have you washed my track suit?'

Oh God, what I'd give for a bit of peace. I knew when I stood up to get that track suit that I wouldn't sit down again that night.

Halfway through rinsing out track suit, my milk comes in. Stuff a bit of toilet paper over nipple in bra, can't stop now, will wait till Rosie yells. Don't have to wait long. Thomas at my heels tugging at my jumper to get there first.

'Go away, and give me peace! I'll die at forty, I know I will.'

Caustic remarks from him, on his way out (done up like a dog's dinner): 'Glad I'm going out tonight!' Afterthought, as he catches look I've thrown, 'Why don't you get an early night?'

(If only I could, craphead!)

I move towards him to kiss him goodbye, breast leaks on his jumper, furious as he rubs at it.

'Oh Christ! Do you have to? Sort yourself out, look at my jumper.'

I want to scream, 'Look at my body!'

Door slams, I sigh and proceed to feed my grappling duo.

'Thomas, you really will have to stop this.' I suddenly have vision of him in school uniform, tearing home for a 12.30 feed. *Yuk*, I'm surprised my breasts don't reach my knees.

'Mum,' a voice breaks into my thoughts. 'Can you help me with my homework?'

Another, smaller, voice, 'Can I read to you?'

'Have you put the button on my school blouse?' Valerie asks.

I say a deflated NO to all three things. 'Let me get these two in bed, then I'll sort you three out.'

Valerie nags on and on about button on blouse, repeating what she has heard him say on occasions, 'What do you do all day?'

She knew she was at a safe distance when she said that. My hand couldn't reach her, and to clout her would have meant dropping two babies to the floor.

Cheeky little bitch. I'll show her. Tomorrow I'll put these two in a taxi and send them to the building site or office, and be out when they come in from school. Even as I thought it, I knew that I wouldn't carry it through.

I feel just about as happy as a dead cat.

I tear both mouths from my sore, tired-looking breasts. Quick examination of them, God they will never be the same again. Attach two nappies to two little bums. In the back of my mind is the nagging thought that they could both do with a bath (soles of Thomas' feet black), but lack vital energy for the mess that it would involve.

Rosie falls asleep almost as soon as her head touches the pillow (must change sheets tomorrow). I stand and gaze at her bald head, willing hair to grow (reluctant to take her anywhere without hat).

Thomas won't give in to sleep at all. Well here goes, have to climb in cot with him again. Haven't yet decided how to get back out, once he's in land o'nod. Climb out with great difficulty. Stirs slightly, I hold my breath, and cross fingers on both hands.

Get told off for falling asleep over homework, not listening to a story, and sewing white button on blue blouse with navy cotton. God am I tired.

13

Can't stand squabbles over whose turn it is to wear the pink nightie and whose hot water bottle leaks. Please go to bed now, before I start shouting. Don't quite manage to count to ten.

'Will you go to bloody bed NOW!' Oh God, it always ends in tears. I hate them to fall asleep crying, haven't got the energy or space in my head to sort it out now. I must make sure that it doesn't happen tomorrow. I've heard myself saying that time and again.

I have to remind myself that I do the best possible job I can, with the resources that are available to me at the time. (A friend told me that once, never forgot it. Mind you, she hanged herself.)

Well here we are, another day nearly over. I list the things in my mind that I do every boring day. Yes that's it, feed the cat and put out the goldfish (well something like that).

I'll have five minutes on the settee, ooh silence is golden, must remember to tuck them all in later on. Hazel is sneezing, can't afford to have that little trouble-maker home from school, never stops teasing Thomas. Stretch, yawn, I feel like the old woman who lived in a shoe. Still, at least I avoided whipping them all. I touch wood quickly, don't quite know why, but my Mum used to.

I awake feeling cold. Stiff neck (head fell over arm of settee, too tired to correct position). Fire's gone out, shit.

Bleary eyes strain at clock. Ten thirty, another day gone.

14

Rosie yelling before I reach bottom of stairs. Please don't wake Thomas, I pray. Too late. Yell, yell, oh well three in a bed again tonight, till he gets in making four. Another night hanging on to mattress by finger nails.

Climb into bed with babes, look down to see breasts fast disappearing down throats of gannets. I'm going to have to give this up, stop biting Thomas, clout across head to no avail.

Both fall asleep, using me as dummy. My eyes close, I'm sure I hear house breathing sigh of relief.

Door slamming wakes me. Draw tiny bodies instinctively closer to me, swinging Thomas' legs over to cover vagina, feign sleep (hopefully authentic).

Small amount of groping, to no avail, wait with bated breath till he turns over. Sleep at last.

It's Thursday tomorrow. Now what shall I do with myself all day? Smile manages to creep over weary face.

Two

Sleepily feel for babies, both fed during the night and are flat out (now it's time to get up). Remember he got up, pulled off top cover from the bed, and went to sleep on settee, announcing, 'I have to work all day, I need my sleep,' as he barged through bedroom door. Bit lip. Need my sleep too, you creep. Bet he goes off to work leaving me to fold the blanket up, I mutter.

Hello, activity next door, must get out of bed before the little crows charge in here like bats from hell and wake these two. Crawl slowly from bed on belly, land on floor in awkward position, stifle an 'ouch'.

Feels good to be eating toast and drinking a cup of tea that's still hot, and in peace too.

He is still asleep when I walk through the living room to switch on radio for correct time (four clocks in house, every one of them says a different time). Blamed me for his being late. Can't quite believe it, scratch my head in amazement, ignore howls of abuse from all quarters, pour second cup of tea.

'There's no sugar on my cornflakes.'

'No,' I answer drily, 'you're getting spots.' (Must

remember to get sugar today, on offer at the Co-op.)

'Where's my clean socks?' yells a voice from somewhere.

'Tried your sock drawer?' I yell back.

He is fighting with the toothpaste, holds up the screwed up, obviously empty tube. 'Think you could remember to get some today? It's not a lot to ask.' (I look away in disgust.) 'I'll have to use salt again.' (There's some slug pellets in the drawer, I mutter, crush them up and try them. Thinks, maybe his bad breath will put Karen off.)

A quick peck on the cheek, and he's gone. 'Good-bye darling,' I shout at the closed door, 'do have a wonderful day.'

'You've got odd socks on Hazel, look the heel of that one is halfway up your leg, that's Val's,' I say, 'probably the one she's turning the drawer upside down for.'

Too late. Val's down and has seen it.

'Get your smelly foot out of my sock.' How aggressive she sounds (like me? I query). 'Mum, tell her, she's got my sock, and I'll be late for school.' More shouts and taunts.

'If I'm late', she screams, 'you'll have to write me a note.'

Oh Lord, anything rather than have to find a scrap of paper this early in the morning.

'Come on love,' I encourage in my best motherly tone, 'If you take it off now, like a good girl (little fiend), Mum will give you 10p to spend on the way to school.'

(The rotten sock is off in seconds.)

'You're always giving her money,' whines Valerie.

17

'Where's mine?' demands Wendy.

I dole 10p out to all three of them, too fed up to argue, and not wanting another scene.

'That bloody sock has cost me 30p,' I moan, checking my purse when they have all left (30p less for food).

I peep around stairs, with ear in direction of bedroom door. This is great, I'll be able to do breakfast dishes and tidy up a little.

I glance around the devastated kitchen. How the heck does it get to look such a pig sty? (Because it houses pigs, came the immediate thought.)

I stop in my tracks, the words of a song on the radio amplified in my head, 'You came into my life, and now you're taking over.' I don't know whether just to smile knowingly, or to kick the bleedin' radio in.

A familiar thudding is heard on the stairs. Thomas always slides down on his bottom.

'Hello son, who's had a nice long sleep then?'

'Milk, milk,' is all he manages to say, tugging at my jumper.

Another day of this, I think, and I'll just open my mouth and scream, and scream, and scream.

I know that if I feed him now, he will demand more as soon as Rosie wakes. This is the latest she has slept for weeks.

I tip up a bucket of bricks on the living room floor to take his mind off feeding, before opening the back door for a quick check on the elements. There is a slight breeze. The dead brambles that I asked him to cut down months ago are gently swaying to and fro at the rear fence in the garden, poking through the spokes on Hazel's rusting bike with the wonky handlebars, that he promised to fix last September. All in all he's pretty useless.

Looks like a good drying day I think, as I gather up all the bits and pieces I can find for a white wash (well, mucky grey in retrospect). A navy towelling jumper found its way into the last white wash a few weeks ago, and I don't think I'll live it down. Thank goodness his new underwear (a present from his lovely Mum) wasn't among it. I shrank that the week after, and have hidden it well, until I can afford to replace it. No wonder it shrank, absolute rubbish – well, what could she buy on the pittance that mean bastard gives her. God is *he* ever a chip off the old block, and what a little love she is. Forty years she has put up with a dog's life, makes me even more determined not to.

There isn't a time when she visits us or we her that she doesn't slip me a quid on the sly. She can ill afford it too, but she's not blind, she sees how I struggle.

The tears well in my eyes when I think of her crumpled, defeated little face every time that pig of a man speaks to her.

Forty years she's had. What a sentence, you would get less than that for murder.

I have to pull myself together, as Rosie's cries sweep down the stairs like thunder bolts. Thomas is there right behind me, as I lift her from cot on to breast. There honestly isn't a place in the house where I can go without at least one child following; my heart goes out to Siamese twins.

'No Thomas, you're not having any. It's got to

stop.' The words have hardly escaped my mouth when a warm feeling begins to spread over the side of my leg. I am completely immobilised with shock. I look at Rosie, convinced she will understand. 'I can't believe it, your brother has just peed on me.'

Thomas edges his way to the door, hands behind back, shrugging shoulders, and tongue popping in and out of his petulant mouth. I glance down at the wet patch on my otherwise clean trousers, and looking towards the ceiling (and Heaven) I ask, almost pleadingly, 'What did I ever do to deserve this?'

Phew! Not a lot to look forward to in Rosie's nappy, by the smell of things.

Laying her, tummy full and contented, on my bed, I make for the bathroom, aware, as soon as my eyes rest on the last toilet roll, shoved as far down the pan as it will go, that it is going to be one of those days.

If I don't get out of the house for at least an hour today, I groan, with rubber-glove-clad hand (with two fingers and thumb missing) squelching desperately in six inches of water, pee and soggy paper, I'll be up for child abuse.

'You can get out of the washing bag Thomas, I'm not going to clout you!' I don't even turn around as I hear the rustle of plastic, and the little feet scurrying back into the bedroom.

If I put it near the gas fire, I think, letting it drip into the bath for a few minutes, it may be dry by the time he comes in, and takes his paper for his usual half-hour, nightly sit-down. I am leaning against the bath holding the disgusting thing in mid-air pulling faces at myself in the somewhat distorted mirror (Woolworth's clearance sale three years ago). I look very jaundiced today, I've always had sallow skin, but today – *yuk*.

Pull down bottom eye-lids, stick out tongue and say 'ah'. Saw a programme on telly yesterday about throat cancer, frightened me to death, reached out for fag to calm my nerves – must give it up, not a good habit to encourage kids in, less harmful to go back to nail-biting. Trouble is I'm twice as horrible to kids when gasping for a cigarette. Leave toilet roll to continue dripping, must investigate too-good-to-be-true silence next door.

'What are you up to Thomas?' I shout from half-way across landing. Scurry of feet again, and banging of drawer. Sitting on the floor trying to hide face under bed when I walk in room. Up to no good, is immediate thought. Takes seconds to find out what he's been up to.

'You stupid boy,' I yell, and before I can stop myself I've belted his backside and dumped him in his cot.

'And why didn't you cry?' I yell at Rosie, who bursts into tears right away at the sound of my cross voice.

Her hands, face and legs, every bit of her that isn't covered, had been drawn on with felt pen.

'You little swine,' I yell again at Thomas, 'you keep this up, and you'll end up in a bloody children's home.' It isn't until much later, when I've calmed down, that I realise what an awful thing that is to say to a child.

I scrub away for ages at Rosie's little body (and, I might add, resist temptation to use Brillo pad), half listening and half choosing to ignore Thomas' frustrated attempts at kicking the cot, knowing that if I go in to him, it will be another clout that both he and I will straight away regret. 'Well Rosie, that will have to do. Any longer in this water, and you'll look like a prune.'

Thomas has given up kicking the cot, and all is quiet. Shoving Rosie under one arm and an assortment of clothes under the other, I creep towards the bedroom and peep around the door. He has fallen asleep all right, but has managed to empty Rosie's talcum powder, shaking it to the four corners of the room. Quick check to see if he's still breathing and hasn't suffocated himself with the stuff, then off I go to dress Rosie in front of the fire, putting yet another needless task out of mind.

I sit down beside a nappy-free Rosie, and watch her trying to kick her little legs. Two-and-a-half months old. Seems like yesterday, I remember the birth with a shudder.

It's a lie that it gets easier with each one.

'Should be like shelling peas to you, dear, by now,' the kindly midwife had patted my shoulder and said. I could have done without hearing that, even though I knew she meant no harm. She was a dear. It just made me feel yet another way in which I'd failed.

I was still looking at Rosie when it occurred to me that it is my/his (our) anniversary next month. Must make sure that the green dress is clean, I thought, as I blew a raspberry on Rosie's bare bum.

Short, sharp taps of rain on the window brought my washing to mind.

'Damn it,' I said out loud, as I dived to the back door. My heart sank when I opened it. The rotten line had broken, the whole of that wash was spread across the grass with muddy bald patches that was our poor excuse for a lawn. I sat down on the wet step, wringing my hands in grief like you would at a funeral.

I heard the clatter of the door knocker while I sat there, chose to ignore it in the hope that whoever the hell it was would go away and leave me to hang myself in peace with the bleedin' washing line.

The knocking was persistent, so I dragged myself through the house to answer it, before it fell off its hinges, and gave me something else to fill my empty day.

'Hello love.' It was Jane with her son James. 'Are you doing anything for the next half hour?' How could I possibly answer that politely.

'Nothing at all,' I heard myself answering caustically. 'Now what would I possibly find to do in this showroom household?'

Jane immediately sussed out what was going on, and put an arm around me. Sympathy always made me cry, and I did just that, blurting between sobs about the broken washing line, bedroom covered in talcum powder, soggy bog roll and Rosie's Maori warpaint.

'Can I use your phone a minute?' she asked, with receiver in hand. I nodded.

23

I was still crying as I put Rosie's clean nappy on, but listened with one ear nevertheless to Jane's telephone conversation.

'Hello, Jane Pepper speaking. I've got an appointment for 11.15 this morning. Yes, that's right, just a check-up. Can I change it to this afternoon sometime? OK, I'll hang on,' she looked my way and winked.

'Pardon? 2.30, great, thanks very much. Bye.'

'What was that all about?' I asked, feeling a bit more composed.

'I was going to ask you to have James for half an hour, while I had my six-monthly check-up at the dentist. I've put it off until this afternoon,' she smiled. 'I'll give you a hand. Where do I start?' she asked. 'Upstairs or down, or,' she added with a giggle, 'in my lady's chamber?'

'We'll start with coffee,' I said, and promptly put the kettle on.

By one o'clock the house was more orderly than it had been for weeks. It was great, too, to be able to feed Rosie without being attacked by Thomas, whose attention was taken with James.

I was always glad to see Jane, she was like a breath of fresh air in my humdrum life. She wasn't a great deal older than me, but had a wealth of experience under her belt. She must have known that I hung on to her every word, even though I tried not to make it obvious.

It was Jane who had made me aware of sexism. I had always felt silent resentment at the way I ran around in small circles after each member of my family, while they in turn snapped their fingers for yet another ounce of blood, and he conducting his demands from the armchair nearest the fire, with the paper under his nose. But until she spelt it out, it hadn't occurred to me to analyse the problem.

I was wondering one evening how low the fire would get before he moved himself off the settee to put on a shovelful of coal. Couldn't believe I'd heard right when he shouted through to me, 'Fire's going out.'

Rosie feeding, Valerie moaning at burning toast (not even attempting to remove from grill), Hazel in sink demanding hair to be rinsed, Wendy in bath shouting for last bar of soap (in sink with Hazel) and Thomas asleep on potty leaning up against back door. Ignored him as he walked through, shaking empty coal bucket. 'This should be filled during the day! What on earth do you do with your time, except drink jars of coffee with that Jane, swopping hard luck stories.'

'There are five children in this house, you know,' my voice was raised in anger.

'Three of them are at school,' he was quick to reply.

I could kick myself, I can never think of a smart answer quick enough for the pig, so each time I lose.

Wish I was as bright and well informed as Jane. She says it's only lack of practice.

It was hard for me to think of her as ever having been browbeaten, although she assures me that she was, and not that long ago.

'There was a time, gal, when I bowed and scraped,

and touched my forelock to his every whim. Then a well meaning friend lent me the *The Women's Room*. I felt so angry that I had to challenge him. That's when the shit really hit the fan. He refused to even take a glimpse at what was going on. I went in with two guns blazing – not recommended, love – so here I am a working mother, free, and as happy as a pig in shit. We have more respect for each other now than all the years we lived together. The man has had to admit that he admires me. It's not easy, though. There have been a few occasions (in moments of weakness) when he's nearly had his shoes under the bed. But I only have to think of his sweaty socks and snotty hankies, and I'm back to reality.'

'What about the kids, Sarah and James, do they suffer?'

'I think they must have, at first. It's confusing, but they appreciate how much more relaxed I am. They don't lie in bed listening to rows any more, trying to be loyal to both of us. It has its compensations too, like two homes and two parents who actually have time for them, only separately. We go out now and then as a family too, and go our own ways when the outing is over.'

How I envied Jane. Every part of her day, awake or asleep, was hers. No lying restless and worried until the early hours of the morning, thinking of his re-action about the latest shrunken item of clothing, or the trousers you haven't pressed, that you know he will want the following morning. Often I would creep out of bed in the early hours and set up the ironing board, knowing that it was the only way to avoid a scene the next day. God, no wonder I felt continually tired and lethargic.

Whatever Jane did was entirely her decision, she frequently told me. 'If I'm wrong about anything, I only have myself to blame, no one else to reinforce the guilt, and if I'm right, I just sit and gloat.'

Listening to Jane, during the day, I really began to believe that I had a life of my own, and the right to expect time to myself. But once she had left the house and he came home, the doubts would come creeping back into my mind.

I smiled as I thought of the first time she had knocked at the door for me during the evening.

'Coming for a swift half up the pub?' she had asked. I went rigid, and nearly wet myself on the doorstep.

'He's in there,' I whispered, pointing to the living room, putting a finger to my lips.

'I'm sure he can hold the fort for half an hour,' she continued.

'I'll get my coat,' I said, quick as a flash, forgetting all about the string of nappy pins dangling from the front of my jumper. I took a deep breath. Here goes!

'I'm popping out with Jane a minute,' I shout into the other room, voice trembling a little.

'What about these kids?' I hear him shout.

'Ignore him,' says Jane, at which I yell, 'Won't be long, love.'

I shook all the way to the pub. Jane was ever so sympathetic, and encouraging.

'You should have done this years ago, love. We set the pattern very early on.'

27

'What will you have?' she asked, striding confidently up to the bar.

'Eh, oh, same as you,' I blurted, sounding the novice I was.

'Mmm, quite nice, what is it?'

'Lager, with a drop of lime to take the bitter edge from it. Good, isn't it?'

I felt as though everyone in that pub was staring at me.

'They're not,' Jane assured me, 'but pull your coat over the nappy pins.'

By the second lager, I was beginning to feel a little less jumpy. 'How long have we been here?' I asked Jane.

'How long is he out on a darts night?' came her quick reply. 'Look, love,' she spoke reassuringly, 'you're not doing anything wrong. Just consider it a lager break instead of a coffee break.'

I was still edgy all the same. 'I ought to be thinking of going soon. Rosie might need a feed.'

Jane just raised her eyebrows, 'Scraping the barrel now, aren't you, love?'

I ran from Jane's house, making sure I saw her door close first, and arrived home breathless and hiccuping. Met with stony silence from him, 'Where have you been?' from Valerie, Wendy and Hazel, bleats from Thomas, and, thank God, sleepy silence from Rosie.

Stayed in the kitchen for a while. Only been gone half an hour, terrible mess. Can't complain though, pushing my luck a bit.

'Fire's gone out in here,' a voice rang out. 'No coal in the bucket again.' Deathly white, gritting teeth, I shout, 'I'm sorting out the kids.'

Didn't stop what I was doing or turn around, as I heard him coming through to the kitchen. He filled the kettle and switched it on.

'For tea,' he said. 'Will you make it when the water boils? And what were you doing at Jane's for forty-five minutes?'

'Just, just' (Christ, I was stuttering) 'just looking at her new duvet covers', I spluttered at last.

'She's always bragging, that one. Don't let it give you ideas.'

I heard him, but was busy smiling to myself and thinking of my outing to the pub. 'The first of many,' I caught myself thinking. A funny excited feeling warmed the pit of my stomach, and didn't go away until Valerie asked me why I was grinning? Pulling myself together, I carried on bathing, feeding and tidying up, until five shiny-nosed kids were in bed.

I was able to sit down by 9.30 that night. Everything had been done with a new zest; I even hung out all evening waiting for him to get up in disgust and make another pot of tea. Felt I might not cook supper either. Did, though, he kicked up such a fuss, said Jane is a bad influence and he might stop her coming to the house. (Wonder if he could?)

Really look forward to Jane tapping at the door, the odd night during the week. Even knocked for her one evening.

He grinned all over his face last night when Rosie woke demanding to be fed, just as we were leaving.

29

'Feed her, then bring her with us,' suggested Jane, took the wind right out of his sails.

Thinking quickly he was. 'You can't take a baby in a pub,' (another grin-cum-sneer).

'We'll go to the club,' offered Jane. 'Kids are allowed in there, part of the policy, family club.'

My knees were shaking.

'How long are you going to be?' he asked drily.

'Not long, the others are ready for bed.'

I could cheerfully have strangled Valerie, as we left: 'Are you going out again Mum? You're always going out.' (What about your father, I was tempted to spit out, but didn't.)

'My life is beginning to change,' I remarked to Jane, while sitting up at the bar, 'but even though I'm getting out of the house, I'm nervous he's going to put his foot down sooner or later.'

'Only if you let him.'

'With the information I have now, I'll never be the same as I was. I can't just pretend that I don't know about sexism. But I'm scared Jane, in case I go too far, and he leaves me.'

'For a start, I don't think he would. You have to take it slowly though. Can't afford to go in with two guns blazing, just because I did. Don't think of the future, and what you haven't got. Concentrate on how well you have done up to now. I know you haven't got him bathing the kids or hoovering; but three months ago you were continually stuck in the house day and night, and now you get out a couple of evenings for the odd hour. And relax, did you ever think you would achieve that?'

'No I didn't, and I don't know what I would have

done without your support.'

'More like bloody incitement, he would say,' quipped Jane. 'He will start saying I'm leading you astray before long.'

'Hey, look at the time, we're starting to get later and later! If there's a sleeping bag on the doorstep when we go down, I'll have to sleep on your settee,' I giggled.

The house was in darkness. I screwed up my face at Jane as I put my key in the lock. I tried to think of the many times when I'd gone to bed, fed up with my own company, but I felt an overwhelming sense of guilt as I laid sleeping Rosie in her cot, and crept into bed beside him. I could tell he wasn't asleep, and he stiffened slightly as I rolled over nearer.

'Sorry I'm late.' I bitterly regretted those words (spoken before I had a chance to think) – I'd never before heard them from him, however late he came home.

He rejected my advances, making me feel like a whore. I had tried to be loving, out of guilt, fear and oppression. I couldn't sleep, for worrying how I could make it better between us.

I was up early the next morning, padding around in the kitchen like a trapped animal, wondering what he would like for breakfast. God! Anything to avoid the silent treatment: it would continue until I admitted that I'd been wrong in going out.

My stomach did a somersault when I heard movement in the room above me. I cast an eye around; tea had been made, toast on the table, cereal out, bacon and eggs ready to hit the pan at a moment's notice.

Please God, don't let him be in a bad mood. I squeezed my hands together, took a deep breath and braced myself for what was to come.

One look at his face and my heart sank. It was the silent treatment.

'Tea's made, love.' My voice trembled. 'I'll pour it now.'

'No thanks, I want to make an early start,' he managed to reply dourly. (At least he had spoken.)

I touched his arm lightly, as he sat putting on his socks.

'It's cold this morning, have a cup of tea and a bit of toast.'

He pulled his arm free, stood up and said, 'I think you had better see to Rosie, I can hear her crying.' His jacket was put on, and he made a move towards the door.

'Don't go off like that, love,' (I could hear myself almost pleading) 'I'll be miserable all day.' (I could have kicked myself, I was begging again.)

He turned at the door (I hoped it was to kiss me goodbye).

'You should have thought about that last night,' was his parting remark, and he was gone, leaving me to another day of torment.

Feeling so bad myself, I was rotten to the children. Poor sods, they couldn't say or do a thing right. Valerie threatened to leave home, waltzing out of the door with an air of indignation, school bag under her arm and marmite sandwiches clutched tightly in her hand. The two younger girls followed their big sister, bursting with support and admiration.

I shuddered as the front door closed behind them. Rosie had cried herself back to sleep. Thomas had taken one look at me and in his infinite young wisdom decided to keep out of my way.

By the time I had cleared the table, and generally tidied up, I could hardly see out of my eyes, they were so swollen. I felt so bloody miserable and beaten.

The phone rang as I pulled Thomas on to my knee to cuddle him in an attempt to make up in some small way for my ranting and raving earlier on.

'Hello.' I hadn't intended to sound as flat as I did. 'Oh, hi, no, I'm fine – well, nothing that a cut throat wouldn't cure.' I paused before admitting, 'Well, he wasn't very happy last night when I got in, and even less friendly this morning. It's going to be another week of rowing unless I apologise soon, throwing myself at his feet, begging to be forgiven, and promising to be a dutiful wife and not step out of line again. I'm so confused,' I went on. 'If I don't go out again, things will eventually settle down. Honest Jane, it's not worth the aggravation, just for a night out.'

Jane hadn't been able to get a word in edgeways up to now.

'Look, I'm going out to lunch today, why don't you join me. It'll do you the world of good.'

I started to make excuses. 'I can't, really. I've got the kids here, there's no one to leave them with. Besides, I thought I'd get the ironing done. I haven't got any money either.'

'You haven't got one valid reason,' she butted in. 'The rotten ironing will always be there, we can take

33

the kids, I'm taking mine, and I'll treat you. I had a postal order from my brother this morning for my birthday. So that seems to be settled. I'll meet you outside the Wagon Wheel at one o'clock.'

She didn't wait for another protest from me, the line went dead. I must say, I felt better already.

I was a bit dubious about taking Rosie and Thomas to somewhere like the Wagon Wheel – I'd had disgusted looks from people in the Wimpy, when orange juice had been spilled over the table and crumbs dropped on the floor. I wasn't at all sure where I felt comfortable, as a working-class mother. It was yet another area in which I was oppressed.

Jane was waiting with Sarah and James when I arrived.

'On the dot,' she smiled, pulling back the sleeve of her jumper to confirm it with her watch.

Rosie had fallen asleep with the movement of the pram, so we were able to push her into a recess near the coat stand, and pick a table not too far away in case she woke.

Even before we could order our meal, James and Thomas demanded to visit the loo and by halfway through the first course they had been four times in all. I was looking in every direction by then, expecting criticism on the face of everyone around me. I was pleasantly surprised to find no one paying us any attention, until James caught sight of a bowl of sugar lumps on the next table. It took a bit of strength and a lot of persuasion from Jane to get him back to his dinner. Then – my face must have been a picture – he stood at the side of his chair, crossed his legs and peed. Jane didn't bat an eye, she walked through to the kitchen for a cloth and quietly wiped it up.

By the time we had finished our pudding Rosie was awake, so it seemed a good idea to go to Jane's for a coffee and not to outstay our welcome in the restaurant. I had cheered up considerably over dinner, but the thought of his long face that evening came flooding back as soon as we approached Jane's.

It was so relaxing in her house, she wasn't carting the hoover about every five minutes, or shouting at the children for dropping crumbs on the floor. There were toys everywhere, we had to move things in order to clear a seat.

'The thing is,' Jane said, as I counted the articles lying around the place, 'children will never remember that you didn't keep the place dusted, but they will remember that you didn't let them have fun. When I was little, my brother and I were only allowed to play with one toy at a time, and that was in the kitchen, never in the living room in front of the fire. "You never know who's going to call and be greeted by a mess," my dear mother used to say. Couldn't blame her though, my father was a real pig. The first thing he used to do at night, when he came home from work, was to run his finger over the sideboard, skirting board and tops of doors, and if he found a speck of dust, he handed her a duster, and asked her what she had been doing all day. I didn't have much sympathy with her as a child, but my God, my heart goes out to her now. I wish I could tell her that.'

'Why, is she dead?' I asked.

'No, she might have been better off dead, who knows? I came home from school one night, just before my fifteenth birthday, and the house was empty. I thought she'd popped out to the shops or something. There was still no sign of her when Dad came in from work. He found a note in the bedroom, it simply said, "Can't take any more, take care of kids, I love them. Helen." I hated her from that moment on. I couldn't understand why she would want to leave us, but it was him, not Allen and me.'

Jane looked so choked. 'Did you ever try to find her?' I asked.

'I did once, but with no success, I don't think she ever wanted to be found. It's quite easy to get lost, if you're determined.' She sighed. 'Maybe I'll try again some day, for the kids' sake, it is their gran.'

'Hey, look at the time,' Jane laughed, 'you had better go and get your dusting done, before the children get in from school.'

I glanced at her clock. 'Three o'clock already. Help! The breakfast dishes are still in the sink.'

I flew from Jane's house like a scalded cat, stopping only to thank her for lunch, and her company. 'See you tomorrow,' I yelled from halfway up the street, 'if I live through tonight, and his mood,' I added with a giggle.

Three

     I couldn't get my mind off Jane's mother. She had to be desperate to walk out on her children. I looked at Thomas and Rosie, and shuddered at the thought of never seeing them grow up.

Valerie was in a good mood when she came in, chatting away to Hazel and Wendy about being picked for the netball team in school. As she passed me in the hall I got a spontaneous kiss, and the coats and school bags were hung up and put away without me having to nag them. What a pleasure that was.

After the afternoon I had spent with Jane, I was determined that, however awful I felt when he came in from work, I wasn't going to run around in small circles to try to please him into being nice to me. Two can play at his silent game I thought, sticking my chin out stubbornly, and what's more it's fish fingers and chips. If he doesn't like it then he can go without. The kids will finish theirs and his.

I felt quite smug about my decision, but at the same time I wasn't sure I wouldn't dash around cooking something else at his first complaint. However determined I seemed now, I wasn't actually facing one of his disgusted 'The cat eats better than that' looks.

My heart started to pound when I heard the car drive up. I waited almost holding my breath for the front door to open and close behind him. I still had made sure that everything was set like the scene in some play or film. Rosie had been fed and was lying contented in her chair in front of the fire, Valerie was finishing her homework in the bedroom, while the other girls were watching television, with Thomas giving his usual running commentary on what he thought was going on.

Oh God here it comes, the footsteps on their way through to the kitchen. Keep your head turned to the cooker, girl, don't shake.

If my lips hadn't been trembling, I might have whistled. What a state to get in, it suddenly dawned on me. I was basically scared of the man! (Oh, perish the thought.)

The coat was hung up on the back door, then, with paper in hand (I presumed, since it had been the same routine for years) he went into the living room for the start of his hard-earned, relaxing evening. (Pisshead! It was wonderful to be able to give vent to my feelings, even if it was only under my breath. Shitface!)

Ten minutes passed and still no sign of him emerging, or speaking (God, ten minutes is a long time). I felt a mixture of relief and sickness, when, without thinking yet again (or was I?), I shouted that his dinner was ready.

I couldn't help but notice the look on his face as his eyes went down to the plate with its three fish fingers, two dozen peas, and a gross of chips.

'What's this then, play-school food?'

'The kids like it,' I quipped defensively, 'it's their favourite. I have to please them sometimes,' I added, trying to justify myself (and for what, I wonder).

'Don't I give you enough money for decent food?' he yelled, moving his chair back from the table.

I faced him this time. 'It's a change,' I challenged.

'And it's a change I can do without,' he argued.

'There are starving people,' I protested, 'that would give anything for a meal like that.'

He removed the plate from the table. (Christ, is he going to throw it at me?)

'Then, I strongly recommend,' he said, putting the plate in my hands, 'that you pack it up and send it to them.'

Left me speechless. Picked up coat, then I heard door slam, and concluded (quite rightly too) that he had gone.

I was amazed to feel an arm around me. I looked up (my head had been laid on the table in despair); it was Valerie.

'Mum, that was a lovely dinner. Dad is probably tired. Don't get upset. I'll make you a cup of tea if you like, Thomas is scribbling on Rosie again,' (all in one breath) 'shall I smack him?'

'No, you pop the kettle on, love, and I'll sort them out.'

Val was so sweet, but I couldn't help noticing the way she had already started to make excuses for her father's bad behaviour. Just like all of us, I thought. Where does it stop? Where have I gone wrong? I've always cooked my own Xmas cake, Xmas pudding, they have always had pancakes on Shrove Tuesday (that's it, they have had too much, and will go on expecting it now until the day I have a stroke).

Thinks: what can I do when he comes in? I know, I'll pretend I'm ill, that usually gets him talking (can't resist asking me if one of the symptoms is morning sickness). Severe tummy pains, must be the coil, I'll say. Doctor's worried about me, I'll add. Better not, knowing him he will phone and check. Oh God, what a state to get into.

Rosie was fed, bathed and bedded. Still no sign of him.

'Come on Thomas, your turn.' I lifted him into the kitchen sink (less mess this way), and threw in a few things for him to float and play with. It felt quite relaxing, not to have him demanding his tea at the same time. Was able to cuddle Thomas while drying him, tell him a story and put him in his cot with a little smile spread over his face as he drifted off to sleep.

Heard the front door shut, so lay down on bed. Must have been there for a good fifteen minutes before he came up: knew he would see my eyelids shake, so turned my head slightly, hardly daring to breathe. Must be standing in doorway looking at me, I thought, since his footsteps didn't cross the room. Stick it out, girl, I know it's uncomfortable, but any second now he will whisper, 'What's wrong, love?'

Very tempted to look up and make first move. Mustn't, will not.

Footsteps coming towards bed. Help! Arm on shoulder.

'What's up with you?' He spoke quietly, so as not

to wake the little ones.

I waited until he asked again, almost spoiling it by giggling (must be nerves).

I made a noise, as if waking from a deep sleep.

'Oh! What! Oh dear! I must have fallen asleep, what time is it?' (I knew damn fine it was shortly after 7.30).

'Aren't you well?' he asked, not really sounding that interested.

'I feel a bit under the weather,' I lied, 'I'm going to have to stay in bed.' My heart was pounding.

'What about the girls?' was his response.

'They can start to get ready for bed. I haven't the energy to get up.'

He wasn't at all pleased – or sympathetic (the pig) – and waited until he got to the door before asking.

'You're not pregnant again, are you?'

Jesus Christ, that takes the biscuit! I had to stuff half the pillow in my mouth to stop myself retaliating and starting a full-scale war.

How the hell does the man think I get pregnant, does he think they fall from above in a heavy shower of rain? Bloody swine, just like his father, who used to make his mother's life a misery when she was pregnant, going on and on at her about being careless.

'He had an accident once love,' she had confessed to me, 'Couldn't manage it for six weeks,' (she had whispered that bit). 'You know what I mean, dear, it was the happiest six weeks of my married life. But he drove me mad when he was fit and able again.

'You know what they say, dear, it doesn't mean much to a woman but we have to do our duty. I

41

always plan the dinner for the next day, that way, with you being occupied, it's over in no time.'

God I felt sick, and guilty for the times that I actually enjoyed and got pleasure from it (mind you they were very few and far between).

Since I planned to stay in bed I might as well get undressed and under the covers. Just about to climb in, knock on the front door, curious, so creep to bottom of stairs. Can hear Jane's voice.

'Oh dear, what's the trouble, shall I go up and see her?'

'No she's asleep, I'll get her to phone you to-morrow.' His tone was very dry. Could have kicked myself all the way up the stairs: have I cut off my nose to spite my face?

Wonder if he will tell me that Jane called, I thought as I lay there. Bet he doesn't. (Cow-fodder. My little terms of endearment for shitface do amuse me, glad he can't read my mind.) Wonder what she wanted? Will ring her if he goes out. My eyes were closing as the words drifted through my mind.

Woke up with a dry throat. Must open the window a bit, forgot earlier on. Could wait here for a fortnight for a cup of tea from him, he wouldn't think to see if I was awake and wanted one, I muttered to myself. Last time he was ill, took a bell upstairs with him. He used it every five bloody minutes too, and me like a little pet dog toddled up and down in response to his every whim. God I must be mad. Was glad to see him recover, what a laugh, he had the flu, and I lost half a stone in weight.

I feel so resentful towards him, could go down and pick a row on the strength of him breathing. Have to count to a hundred.

House appears to be in darkness. Quick check on girls, what a mess, wouldn't think of hanging clothes up unless I remind them, wouldn't occur to him to remind them either. I'm not picking them up, they can go crumpled to school. End up folding them on chair, thinking it is a reflection on me (mug again).

What a sight to greet me in the kitchen. Dirty dishes stacked in sink, sink half full of cold water, toothbrushes dropped in it, plus soap and two rounds of soggy burnt toast. It's never going to change.

Dialled Jane's number, waited a while, receiver picked up at last.

'Hello Jane, was that you at the door tonight? No, nothing serious, just felt tired, I've only just got up to make a cup of tea. Did you go out?' I asked. 'Good play, oh is there? I'll switch it on then, see you tomorrow, bye.'

Television on, kettle on, log on fire, umm, cosy. No it can't be! Went to bottom of stairs, ran up two at a time, got to bedroom before Rosie managed to wake Thomas. Don't really mind her on her own: once fed, she will lie on my knees asleep or at least contented for a while. Can still get to watch a programme in peace. Had a quick look at sink again, chose to ignore it until morning, pulling gruesome face in its direction.

There were so few times in my life when I could give one child all my attention; I had usually to spread myself so thinly that what time there was available

43

for a single child was too short to be of much use. This was nice, being able to caress and play with Rosie uninterrupted. She responded by looking up at me with such trust and dependency.

It's hard work keeping track of five children, with no help. Some evenings I've been so physically and mentally worn out that I've ended up washing some of them twice, and others not at all.

I had this vision in my mind once (brought tears to my eyes) of the Von Trapp children, all lined up, looking spendid in the new clothes Maria had made them out of some old curtains. Mine never looked like that (bit of a sight they'd be in Regency stripe and bathroom towelling, anyway).

Whenever one of mine looked 'well turned out', there was always another sticking out like a sore thumb (the next in line for the goodies), in trousers at half-mast, sleeves of jumpers finishing at the elbows, shoes down at heel. Wish I could afford to have them all well clothed at the same time. Never mind, I console myself, Red Cross parcels didn't do me any harm.

What's that smell? God the kettle! Fling back door open to let out smoke, fling kettle after it. That's the second one this month.

Ah well, back to saucepans. Shan't tell him, say it's lost. Surprising how many things get lost in this house. Have to get one this week from somewhere, his parents are coming at the weekend (more expense – but don't begrudge *her* anything, must add).

If I can fiddle a bit with the housekeeping money, I'd like to take her out to lunch one day, sure Jane would have the young ones for me. She would like that, Gertie. Wonder when was the last time she ever had a special treat? Oh God, she'd probably wear the gold lamé cardigan. Brings it with her every visit, never had the chance to wear it yet, and it's ten years old. Quite excited, thinking about how she would enjoy herself.

'What about the men?' she would say, 'Shall we leave them some sandwiches, or shall we cook for them before we go?'

'Well Gertie my love,' I say out loud, grinning from ear to ear, 'we will do neither. You're going to see some changes in me this time, and, if I'm right, your knees may give way at some point, but on the other hand it will warm the cockles of your heart.' I sniggered at the thought of his prison warder father's face as Gertie and I swan arm in arm out of the house.

Damn and blast, the saucepan. Saved in the nick of time, can explain missing kettle, but not pan as well.

Success at last. Forty-five minutes to make a cup of tea.

Key in lock. Hello, he's in, early too, wonder where he's been? It will annoy him more if I don't ask him, so I shan't.

'You look a bit better,' he says, plonking himself in chair, 'have a good sleep?' (Thinks: sounds pleasant, for him.)

'Wouldn't have got up, but Rosie woke me. Easier to feed her down here than wake the other crows.'

'Fancy a cup of tea?' he asked. (Ooh, things are looking up.)

'Don't mind if I do.'

'Stick the kettle on then love, while I go to the toilet.'

Well I'm buggered, I've heard it all now. I knew there had to be a catch in it somewhere.

'Didn't you put the kettle on?' he asked when he came back down.

I answered him without even looking up, 'No, I can't find it.'

'Can't find it? What do you mean?' He began to raise his voice, 'How the bloody hell can you lose a kettle, woman?'

I don't know how I contained myself.

'Well,' I stuttered, 'I haven't actually lost it, I slung it in the garden.' (Here goes: you've burnt it, haven't you? My God, woman, that's two in six months, and it's me that has to earn the money to replace the things that you're so bloody careless with. Stomp, stomp, up the stairs to bed.)

He was right on cue (thumping great predictable bore).

'You've burnt it, haven't you? My God, woman, that's two in six months and it's me that has to earn the money to replace the things that you're so bloody careless with!' (and he did stomp up to bed).

Ah! If it wasn't painful, I'd tear my hair out.

'Come on Rosie, nappy change, and we'll follow the old swine up the apples and pears.'

It had never occurred to me, that is until Jane pointed it out, that a woman can and should class half of a man's earnings as her own. After all is said and done, if it wasn't for you looking after his children (she never uses the word 'kids', says its oppressive to young people. Must try to stop the habit myself, it means 'baby goat') he wouldn't be able to go out to work. Up to recently I was convinced that everything in the house was my work, and that I should be grateful if and when he slipped me a few extra quid (wonder if Jane thinks that 'quid' is oppressive to a pound note?). Because of my confusion, I tend to fall more easily into the victim role.

I may not change a lot, or quickly, but I'll never be the same as I was. Understanding, once grasped, can never be retracted. And I am beginning to feel fairly desperate; I have to do something, even if it's just getting some financial independence.

How the heck can I work with five children, two of them breast-fed? I'm too tired to think now, I'll leave it until the morning.

Valerie was shaking me to consciousness.

'Mum, my goldfish is missing, do you think Smudge. . .' (the cat, scabby-looking individual).

'Val, it's seven o'clock, go back to bed!'

'But Mum,' she sobbed, 'I like that fish, I spent £2 winning it at the fair.'

'I spent £2 you mean.' I rolled over, and tried to drift off, but it was clear by the way she tore the covers from me that I wouldn't be able. I dragged myself out of bed, putting a finger to my lips and pointing in the direction of the two babes, while reaching bleary-eyed for my dressing gown.

'Didn't your father put wire over the top of the bowl?' I asked on the way down the stairs.

She nodded, her eyes filling with tears.

The wire was still in place on top of the bowl, but the wretched fish nowhere to be found. Valerie had me looking in the most unlikely places, by this time in quite a state.

'No, Valerie, it wouldn't be in the fridge, nor in the cutlery drawer. Be sensible, love, how could it get in the bread bin?'

'You never loved that fish,' she ranted, 'that's why you're not looking properly!'

I turned my head away. I couldn't let her see me laugh.

'That cat's had him,' she yelled, 'he had the budgie!'

'If you hadn't been practising the kiss of life on the poor bird, and blowing so hard down its beak, it wouldn't have been weak enough to fall off the pelmet on to the floor in the first place,' I yelled back, a vivid picture of blue feathers everywhere, and no bird, flashing into my mind.

'Well, Val, it's not anywhere to be found, love. Just forget about it and get ready for school.'

She crossed her arms, sat on the stairs like a picket, and declared in her most defiant tone, 'I'm not going to school until that fish is found.'

I knew only too well that she meant it, and squeezed past her up the stairs to get dressed.

He opened one eye, and asked what was wrong, as I went into the bedroom.

'The goldfish is gone.'

'Well, the cat's had it then,' he replied.

'Wire's still on top of the bowl,' I told him.

'Well, the water's filthy, probably couldn't see it if it was there. Looked underneath the weed?' He laughed. I smiled too.

'Valerie isn't at all amused, and is threatening to stay home from school until the blessed thing is found.'

48

He got up and went down to see Valerie.

'Come on, love,' he said encouragingly, 'I'll help you look.'

I heard the taps going, and guessed that he must have been emptying the bowl into the sink, in a thorough search for the little critter.

Rosie and Thomas hadn't stirred, so I crept down to join them peering through the weeds in their fruitless quest.

'Do you think this is a case for Sherlock Holmes?' I quipped, wishing I hadn't when I received icy glares from the pair of them.

'The ruddy thing isn't here, Val,' he announced a full ten minutes later, beginning to prod into the water at random with both hands.

She ran up the stairs, and I guessed by the thud, threw herself on to her bed, probably sobbing. I didn't follow, I let him go up to her.

'What's wrong with our Val, Mum?' Wendy asked, padding into the kitchen.

'The goldfish has gone, love, think the cat's had it.'

Her little face went stark white, and she burst into floods of tears. 'I took it to school for nature study on Monday,' she wept.

'Well that's all right, then, what a relief. I'll tell Val, and you can bring it home tonight.'

'Don't tell Val,' she shrieked, 'I forgot to give it to teacher, and it's still in my coat pocket.'

My stomach, and my heart, turned over together. 'You what?'

'Oh don't be angry, Mummy. I can't bear it. I couldn't find a jam jar, I ran to school to put it in the sink when I got there, but I forgot by the time I got in the play-yard.' She burst into sobs again.

'Sh, sh, don't let Val hear you. Where is it now?'

'Still in my coat pocket.' Her lips trembled as she spoke.

'Look, this is going to have to be our secret. I'll get rid of it. You go and dry your eyes now. We won't ever tell her, I'll get her another one at the market today.'

Wendy flung her arms around me, almost stopping my breath.

She went into the toilet, giving her nose a few sharp blows, leaving me to deal with the contents of the coat pocket.

I shivered as I put my hand in, and felt sick when I saw the thing, eyes and mouth wide open as if gasping for air (probably was at some point, poor little sod), cold, black, stiff and stuck fast to a half sucked Victory V. What a way to go, I thought as I flushed it down the toilet in one fell swoop.

'I've promised her another goldfish,' he said, handing me a £1, 'will you get it today? She's getting ready for school.'

I nodded. Bloody great, he makes the promises, I have to keep them. Still, anything to calm her down.

Jane was hysterical when she came round for a cuppa later on that morning, and I told her the saga of the fish and bird. She almost fell off the chair.

'Oh I can't help it,' she said, tears rolling down her cheeks, 'I know this is sick, but I can't help wondering what the cat's fate will be.'

We both looked at him, stretched out in front of the fire, his face showing no expression at all as we split our sides.

'It's a bit pathetic, isn't it, when a dead goldfish and budgie provide the only humour in my life?'

'Is it him?' Jane asked.

'I just feel so mixed up. I don't now whether to be angry with myself, angry with him, or with my mother for leading me to believe that all life had in store for me was being a wife and mother. She never once encouraged me with my school work, but sat with my two brothers night after night relentlessly until they both made it to college. "It's not import-ant for a girl, love. Girls grow up and get married, and look after their man and their home and their children. Better for you to learn how to manage housekeeping money like I do. Your father has never had any complaints. And good cooking is essential, you know, good home cooking, a hot meal on the table ready for them when they come in after a day's work." The last bit always got me Jane. I remember it word for word. The way to a man's heart is through his stomach.'

'God, doesn't it make you sick? As far as I can see, the way to a man's heart is with a pissing pick-axe.'

'Do you know Jane, even when my father died there was no peace (God rest his black soul) for her. She got herself in debt to give him the kind of funeral he would have approved of. It took her five more years of slaving in posh houses for other people to pay for that swine's death. I never knew, she kept it from everyone, until she made the last payment, and brought half a bottle of sherry home to celebrate. He

51

controlled her life even beyond the grave.'

'It might be too late for your mum, but it isn't too late for you,' Jane answered firmly. 'You have to consider your four girls, you know, as well as yourself: in twenty years' time there could be four more submissive women, warming four pairs of slippers by the fire for four little men who will demand dinner on the table at the same time every night.'

I stood aghast for a moment. 'Jane, how can I stop it happening, I feel so powerless. As soon as I make the slightest change (or try to), I feel guilty.'

'It's a trap that we all fall into, even I do. You can't expect generations of brainwashing to be wiped out in a week. Men have been brainwashed too, you know, they are not aware of how badly they behave to women. There are very few men that aren't sexist on at least some level.'

Jane seemed to have all the answers.

'Whenever I'm with you, Jane, I feel supported, but when I'm on my own with him the doubts crash in on me. He can be so nasty, it makes my life so miserable, that I feel as though it's easier to carry on being a drudge than fight against it and him. It feels like I'm taking on the whole world and no one will ever understand. The worst bit is the desperate emptiness that seems to be the biggest part of my existence. Oh Jane,' I said, even sounding desperate now, 'I just can't explain how I feel, it's like a huge permanent itch on my back that I can't scratch.'

Jane smiled, 'Don't think I haven't felt the very same itch, I have. I've felt at times that it might be easier to give up or die, but we didn't get the vote by women killing themselves, we got it by fighting and unity. The very women that we think are bores because they're so submissive, those are the ones we are fighting for. They're not bores, they are submissive but not through choice. They haven't had a choice in their lives. They are merely doing what has been expected of them, as their mothers and grandmothers before them have done.'

Her voice became quite intense. 'If as women we feel we can't support each other, it's because we are going on internalising our own oppression. Women fighting other women instead of supporting them keep the system ticking over very nicely. That's what it has always been doing, keeping women as far apart as possible, so that our only models of support are men. So it goes on, and will continue, unless we all do our share of disrupting the balance of power.'

'Jane,' I interrupted her, 'I'm not as intelligent, or as strong as you. At the moment I feel as though I would do anything for peace.'

'I'm not more intelligent, love, I just have a little bit more information than you, and I've been in the war a little longer, that's all. Last, but not least, I don't have a man's resentment and oppression running at me twenty-four hours a day, which I must admit gives me a lot more breathing space. You mustn't give up every time you lose a small battle; battles are being lost everywhere. It's important to hold in your head that it's the war we are after. What's the worst thing that you fear could happen to you, if you keep on fighting?' Jane asked after a pause.

'I suppose,' I answered slowly, 'that he might leave me.'

'What is worse,' she asked again, 'living with him in misery, or without him?'

'It's not even him,' I sighed, 'it's the children, in case he ever tried to take them from me. A lot of men recently have won custody of their children in the courts.

'I have visions,' I went on, 'of him standing in court with a male solicitor, telling a male judge that I'm involved with Women's Lib, and that I'm making him and the children's lives a misery. I just can't bear to think about it.'

'I know what you mean,' Jane said quietly, 'Larry threatened that. It's very rarely they carry it through, it's much more convenient for a man to have access to his children than custody; the price is usually too high for a man to become by choice a full-time parent. But that fear alone in the back of a woman's mind keeps the oppression going; don't you see what I mean?'

'I do, Jane, but I'm haunted night and day by thoughts of what it would be like without my children. I think I would rather kill us all.'

'Scores of women do that too, poor cows, without ever trying to fight.'

'Jane, I don't want to leave him, there's a lot about the man that I love. But I can't go on feeling this awful. I can't even ask for money without him making it seem like the crime of the century.'

'Haven't you thought about earning your own money?' she asked.

'What could I do with five children? Besides, I've never had any training in anything.'

'Hey, that's a defeatist attitude, there's got to be

some way for you to earn a few bob. I'll support you all I can. That includes not coming round in the evening so frequently, for a while anyway. I'm sure your old man thinks that I'm a bad influence on you. But two heads are better than one. We can start from now, thinking about ways to earn some cash, and on a regular basis too.'

'Do you still feed information into computers?' I asked

'Yes, and damn good at it too I am,' beamed Jane. 'It really suits me, my work. I can pick my own hours, take the children with me when they are off school, holidays etc. Wouldn't be without it.'

'You're lucky being able to type well,' I said with envy, adding, 'actually they were advertising at the school for cleaners last week. I wonder if the vacancies have been filled?'

'That's no good,' Jane butted in, 'you have to set your sights higher than that. All you will be doing is going from one cleaning job to another. No, we will have to come up with something more ambitious than that. You want to try to do something free-lance, that you can work in with school and a baby-minder or something.'

'What about one of the supermarkets? They're always advertising for evening workers, filling shelves, etc.'

'Yuk.' What a face she pulled. 'You deserve better than that.'

Another bright idea came to me, 'What about night duty in one of the hospitals, looking after old people or something?'

Jane ruled that out too. 'No,' she said with a wave

of her hand, 'very commendable, I'm sure, but glorified cleaner again. Besides, you're looking after semi-invalids now. You have to get right away from the syndrome you're in, you want to work at something stimulating, or it isn't worth bothering at all.'

'Right boss,' I said, giving her a mock salute, which tickled her pink.

'Well,' she said at last, at the end of a long thoughtful look. 'It isn't imperative that we come up with the answer today. At least it's got you thinking, taken your mind off your miserable existence for five minutes,' she laughed.

'Don't think you realise how much better I feel,' I said, seeing her to the door. 'Honestly, Jane,' I couldn't help the tears, 'you have given me something to hope for, I feel quite excited. Even the thought of him opposing it' (which I knew he would) 'doesn't put a damper on my spirit.'

I spent the rest of the day in the park with Thomas and Rosie, sticking two fingers up to the ironing pile and the fluff on the carpets. It's got to be the best day of my life, a spring in my step, flutter in my tummy, and my head and heart pounding with enthusiasm. Yahooey!

Four

     I met the girls from school, delighted looks on their little faces, spent my last 50p on four ice lollies, and didn't bat an eye when Thomas trod dog-shit right through the house. God if this is happiness and contentment, give me more.

The girls were great with Thomas while I fed Rosie. Hope he loses interest in my breast soon. That would be one off my back (or should I say front?).

Surprised him by kissing him when he came in, bursting to tell him. But not yet, must hang on until something definite happens. It doesn't matter how rotten he is tonight, I thought, he won't bring me down off my cloud.

He was really pleasant all evening, and during Rosie's late night feed he reached for his coat.

'Fancy some fish and chips?' he asked, turning to me.

'Love some, I'll make some tea while you're gone,' I offered.

We didn't bother with the late night film, we went to bed early and made love. It's so good when we are getting on well, he's so gentle and considerate. I wish it could be like this all the time. Even my suspicions of him having an affair with Karen were pushed to the back of my mind as we lay there closer to each other that we had been in quite some time.

I even wondered if I had been presumptuous in wanting some financial independence, but I slept well all the same.

Hoorah, another night without Rosie waking for a feed. Breasts are a bit engorged, but this feed should settle them down.

'Ouch Rosie, wish you hadn't cut that tooth so early.'

Kissed my cheek, as he passed Rosie and me.

'I'll put the kettle on, love, give you a shout when tea is made.'

He's so lovely, I thought, even when he shouted up the stairs, 'The girls want their breakfast, love.'

It didn't take a lot from him to make me happy. Whenever he was pleasant, I almost forgot about the times when things were really awful.

Amazing how one can plummet from elation to depression in around half-an-hour flat.

I scanned the kitchen after he had left the house. He had fried an egg, and made a cup of tea.

I had to scrape the fossilised remains of the ruptured yolk from the frying pan (leaving it to soak for at least an hour), scrub at the stains his soggy tea bag made on the draining board (we do have a bin in the kitchen, maybe it needs a label on it), and take a

Brillo pad to the layer of fat on the tiles at the side of the cooker.

I can't win. Even when a member of my family decides to do something for themselves, there is such a mess for me to clear up after them that it's easier to do it myself in the first place.

'Where's the eggs?' they shout (always have been kept in the bottom of the fridge). 'Where's the milk?' (next to the eggs). 'Where's the . . .?' They know that at this point I'll leave whatever I happen to be doing and take over.

I remember the time I left Rosie with him to do some shopping in peace. Her legs were nearly dis-jointed when I got back: he couldn't find a nappy, and had used a bath towel instead (useless bloody creature).

If I did take a job, I had well-founded suspicions that the whole of the house would become a dis-organised wreck, or I would be lying in a psychiatric wing of a hospital inside a month.

But I was determined to give it a try, even with these thoughts weighing heavily on my mind.

With renewed enthusiasm, I whipped around my daily chores, and after settling Thomas in front of the television in time for Play School (which always provides me with a half-hour breather) and putting Rosie down for her morning nap (she was sleeping more and more infrequently), I sprawled out on the floor with the paper open at Situations Vacant – only to be interrupted seconds later by the phone.

'Can you pop down for a cup of coffee?' asked Jane.

'I've just got Rosie settled,' I replied. 'Why don't

you come up here? See you in a couple of minutes.'

I couldn't help wondering why she sounded so lively, unless she had found the ideal job for me.

Jane was grinning from ear to ear when she arrived.

'You know that party that I've been invited to on Saturday?' she enthused. 'Well, I was going to go, but his lordship will be there, if he knows I'm going; and if I know him as well as I think I do, he will be throwing himself at women all night – he thinks it makes me jealous, in fact it makes him look stupid. Well I told Connie, the girl whose birthday party it is, that I wouldn't be going, but I've changed my mind. I thought of a plan of action in bed last night. He will be furious!'

'Sounds ever so confusing,' I said, handing her coffee to her.

'I'm going to phone one of those agencies, you know, Dial-a-Date or something, to get a man for the evening. It will shock him rigid, put a stop to his little caper for a while, eh?'

'You wouldn't,' I said, amused, but vaguely nervous at the very idea of it. 'You won't know if you're going to get the right type. If it's done by computer you could end up with a sixty-year-old, balding professor who spent the whole evening boring you to death with the life cycle of the female fly, or . . . what the heaviest snowfall ever recorded was.'

'Ah, I already thought of that, so here are the details of me to put into the computer: attractive fun-loving blonde,' she began.

'Hey!' I interrupted, 'If I did that, you would say

it was playing into sexism.'

'I know,' she said, pulling a face, 'but I thought it wouldn't do any harm, just this once. I wonder if there's an agency for male hookers anywhere?'

I could see Jane was rapidly going off the idea.

'Have I dampened your spirits?' I laughed.

'Hey, how about trying a theatrical agency?' I offered. 'You could get a list of them in the library. What sort of man do you want anyway?'

'Well, something that would make him look twice. I'd make it clear that sex was out of the question, and that I'd just want him to be very attentive all evening, then we would slide away from the party early, making sure we were a safe distance away before I paid him, and we went our separate ways. Can you imagine the look on his face?' she shrieked. 'The satisfaction I would get from doing something like that would be worth fifty quid to me. I've just had another thought,' she laughed, 'we could start our own agency, Rent-a-Man.'

We both fell about. 'Rent-a-Man! Ha ha, Rent-a-Man! You can't give em away.'

This line of banter kept us laughing most of that morning. Needless to say Jane never did hire a man, and didn't bother going to the party.

Even when the pump broke on the washing machine that afternoon, I felt in spirits adequate to cope with it and the mess it created.

Damn glad he was at work when the plumber arrived a few days later; could have kicked him the way he spoke down to me.

'You really must empty trouser pockets before putting them in the machine,' he said, handing me an assortment of screws, pennies, and even a wheel off one of Thomas' Dinky toys.

'You women are all the same,' he nattered on. 'If I had my way, wouldn't allow a woman to go near a piece of machinery, always buggering them up for men to repair.'

I think I would have kicked him in the groin if I hadn't turned my back and walked away from him instead. (Bloody moron.)

I had an instant picture of his poor wife on bended knees, thanking him for allowing her to breathe in the same room as him.

That's it, if he's here an hour, shan't make him a cup of tea.

'Are my brown trousers clean?' my lord and master asked that night (resisted temptation to say, 'You should know better than me, you wear them,' God! Wardrobe mistress as well).

Smiled sweetly and said, 'Don't know, dear.'

'Could you get them ready for tomorrow night?' he asked.

'Yes, dear.' (Washed, dried and pressed in a day, your word is my command.) Where's he going tomorrow? I wondered. Didn't dare ask.

Had a terrible evening with Rosie, couldn't settle her all night, put my finger in her mouth, feels like another tooth coming. Oh no, my poor breasts! It was then that I decided I was going to wean her as soon as I could. I had been breast feeding continually for two-and-a-half years, my body wasn't my own! Besides (guilt creeping in), if I was going to be serious about working, I wouldn't want leaking or engorged breasts to contend with.

Yuk! pulling face in bathroom mirror, look and feel washed out. Rosie awake most of the night, I hate teething almost as much as she does. I'll be glad when she has all of them. Think I'll have a hot bath to relax me before she wakes up again, and everyone else does.

I'll use the sachet Jane gave me yesterday. Mm, smells nice; ooh, this is lovely.

'Is that you, love?' There is a tap on the bathroom door.

I should have guessed someone would find me. 'Just a minute.'

Soaked floor answering door, splashed in again. If it's his breakfast he wants and not the toilet, he can bloody well wait.

He just stood there with a grin on his face.

'What's up with you?' I asked, 'Won the pools? What's that behind your back?

'Roses! What for? Where did you get them?'

'Have you forgotten what day it is?' he grinned, 'it's usually me that has to be reminded. It's our anniversary!'

'So it is, where on earth did you hide the flowers?'

'In the broom-cum-rubbish cupboard under the stairs. I'm surprised they survived,' said he, giving them a quick inspection, 'but they did.'

'They're lovely.' I took them in my soapy hands.

'That's the first time in twelve years you have remembered.'

I was quite touched.

'I've arranged with Jane for her to have the kids tonight, so that we can go out for a meal.'

'She didn't mention it yesterday, you secretive pair!' I almost spoilt it by saying, 'She's all right for baby-sitting then, but not as my friend.' I didn't bother, I was looking forward to this meal, and busy thinking of the succulent steak.

Tonight would be a good opportunity to tell him of my plans to get a job; a restaurant would be a good setting for that bombshell.

Jane turned up early. She knew that I would have to get all five ready for bed unaided, and had come to give me a hand.

'Don't want you to be too worn out to enjoy that steak,' she smirked, pointing to him dozing in the chair.

'I'll put my two in your bed when they're tired, if that's OK with you, until you get back. I'm in no hurry mind,' she added with a wink. 'Make the most of it, choose the most expensive things on the menu, you probably won't go out for another year.'

(She was right, but I didn't.)

We went to a new restaurant out of town, The Cabana it was called. The decor was really something, and, by the prices, we were probably paying for that as well as the food.

We were halfway through the first bottle of wine when I thought I would tell him that I would like to get a job. I was careful how I put it, saying that I had thought about it rather than that I was determined to work.

'Why do you want to work?' was his response. 'Most people look forward to retiring. You house-wives don't realise when you're well off, being at home. Life of Riley you've got,' he said, chewing a lump of steak.

I nearly choked on mine, and reached for my wine glass.

'Why don't you help out at the playgroup if you're bored, and have time on your hands? That would be just your cup of tea, being with kids all day, keep you out of mischief,' he winked.

I nearly bit a piece out of the glass.

'I don't want to work with children,' I said, trying to keep my voice calm, 'I want to get away from children, for a few hours a day.'

'You should have thought about that before you had them.' He stuffed another piece of steak in his gob (tempted to ram fork down after it).

I smiled politely. 'It did take the two of us to produce them dear, or was it a recurring illness I got?'

He didn't stop stuffing himself to answer.

'Another reason for me working,' I began, 'is to have some money of my own, a bit of independence.'

The expression on his face changed. 'You can cut that out,' he said, putting the knife and fork down to point at me.

'That's that bloody Jane and her Women's Lib. I won't have it in my house, so you can think again, woman, your job is in the home.'

He had kept his voice fairly quiet and calm up to

now, but I knew it was only a matter of time before everyone in that restaurant would be staring in our direction.

This wasn't the time nor place to challenge him, and I sincerely wished right then that I hadn't started. It was definitely going to have to wait, but give up I wasn't going to do.

I ate the rest of my meal in silence, which I think he took as his triumph and my defeat.

We'll see, I thought, we'll see.

Apart from my lychees (usually my favourite sweet, and these were fresh, not tinned) sticking in my throat a bit, I tried my best to relax for the rest of the evening. I even made a toast with the third bottle of wine.

'Well dear,' (knocking his glass with mine), 'here's to the next twelve years!' (Fought hard against saying, 'Hope they're as happy as the last', although I wanted to say 'here's to change, and my freedom'.)

My main worry as the end of the meal drew closer was the drive home. Even as the thought went through my mind, as if by telepathy, he called the waiter and asked if he could phone for a taxi.

I breathed a sigh of relief, thinking of narrow escapes in the past.

We cuddled together in the back of the cab, and I knew what to expect when we got home. I felt as though in some way I owed it to him, after he had spent so much money on the meal, although I could quite readily have fallen into bed and slept like a log.

Things at home had gone smoothly for Jane, and Rosie, who had been given the last drop of my expressed milk just before we arrived back, looked as though she was settled for the night. His eyes lit up, my heart sank.

Ah well, suppose I must do my bit for England, I thought, bidding Jane a thank you and goodnight.

I dragged myself, three parts cut, up the stairs. Every time I hiccuped I could taste a mixture of lychees and wine.

It had been a long time since I'd been such an eager reciprocator in our lovemaking; I was usually too worn out. Whether it was the wine, the fact that I knew Rosie wouldn't wake up, or the good evening we had spent together, I don't know, but I seemed to float away in ecstacy. He could be so very tender. As I lay in his arms when we had finished, I felt convinced that our marriage would last for ever.

I was wakened with a cup of tea in bed. I felt like Sleeping Beauty as he leaned over and gently kissed me. Maybe I should be lively in bed more often, I thought, if it gets me this sort of treatment.

Rosie and Thomas were still out of the game; four nights in a row, this was a record! I sat there drinking my tea in glorious peace. I'd never much liked tea in bed (usually managed to stain the sheet), but I wasn't about to tell him that.

'The buckle's hanging off my shoe,' Wendy ran yelling into the bedroom to tell me.

'And I can't find my gym shorts,' added Valerie.

In an instant my peace was shattered. Thomas, with the sleep still in his eyes, was banging down the side of one cot, and a little head was moving about in the other one.

With some difficulty (although plenty of practice) I managed to sew on the buckle, feed Rosie at the same time, shout to Val places to look for gym shorts, and keep my cool, to boot.

Nine fifteen, and the house was plunged into silence. Will relax with second cup of tea before attempting to spread some order around disaster area.

Can still taste lychees when I burp.

My heart leapt, when I saw the advert in the paper: *Bingo Caller, three afternoons a week.* There was a phone number, and before I'd given the matter any thought at all, I was dialling it.

I rubbed my hands together excitedly, and then phoned Jane.

'Hi, it's me, are you working this afternoon, or could you have Thomas and Rosie for half an hour? Yes OK, no, I'll tell you when I get there. It's an interview for a job, but I'm not telling you any more than that.'

I grinned as I put the phone down. If I know Jane, she won't be able to contain herself until I get there and tell her all about it.

I took the navy coat from my wardrobe, the one I had bought to go on honeymoon. It had looked smart at the time, very fashionable, brightened up with powder-blue accessories. But now it hung limply over my arm, looking its age with faded cuffs and hem. I slung it with a disgusted sigh back into the bottom of my wardrobe, and reached for my anorak, at the same time peering out of the window for quick check of weather. If it doesn't rain this will do. Scrape at whatever stain that is down the front and across one pocket – take a cloth to it when I go downstairs.

So long since I went for an interview, forgotten how to dress, or act. Had to keep reminding myself, it's only a bingo hall, love, not the Ritz. Still felt nervous.

Went to the toilet four times in fifteen minutes, and again when I arrived at Jane's.

'What's all this then? Got time for a coffee?' asked Jane, all in one breath.

Declining her offer of coffee (I would end up in the loo again), I shoved the paper in front of her face. I had left it open at the ad page.

'What do you think of that then?' I asked enthusiastically.

She didn't seem as pleased as I thought she would be, but I put that down to Thomas and James squabbling over a toy – once they started it was enough to distract a saint.

She wished me luck, saying that if I wasn't back by 3.30 she would make her way to my house in time for the girls coming home from school.

'Do I look all right?' I asked, as she shoved me through the door.

'Great,' she yelled, 'don't come back unless you've got it!'

The local cinema, which had turned to bingo in the afternoons for bored housewives, was just a short walk away in the centre of the shopping precinct. I went straight in (quite bravely, I thought), and tapped at the door marked 'Manager'. A young man answered (they get younger and younger, don't they?) and beckoned me in.

There were half a dozen people sitting there already, and two more followed me, all hoping to get the job, I presumed.

The manager talked collectively to us for a while, asked us a few individual questions, took our names and addresses, then said he would make a short-list and send for the lucky ones within a day or two.

That was it, all over, and very painless. I was even inclined to feel sorry for one or two of the women, who looked to be desperate; but there were only three vacancies, and I really wanted one.

I was back at Jane's by five to three: there, interviewed and back in twenty-five minutes.

'He's going to make a short-list,' I explained to Jane, 'and then send for the lucky ones, who will then go in for an afternoon, to listen to one of the callers to get the hang of it.' I sipped away at my coffee, very preoccupied with my anxiety about getting that job, Thomas and Rosie mauling me at the same time (God, you would think I'd been away for a month).

I felt smug when he came in that evening. Didn't dare risk telling him yet, since I might be causing a scene for nothing if in the end the job was given to someone else (already sewn up the baby-sitting with Jane, there's optimism).

The chance of getting out of the house and meeting people three afternoons a week cheered me up to such an extent that I went out of my way to be patient and pleasant to the children. Even when

Thomas walked his egg right through the living room, getting yolk on the furniture as well as the television screen, it didn't occur to me to shout at him. There were three drinks within half an hour all over my really done-in carpet, but that too was wiped up with no snide remarks or sore bums. Gosh, if it's like this in theory, what's the real thing going to be like, with wages too! I rubbed my hands together gleefully, much to the surprise of the children, who exchanged 'Mum's-gone-crazy' looks amongst themselves.

That evening, Wendy got her buckle properly sewn in place on her shoe, Valerie got her gym shorts (in shoe cupboard), Thomas and Hazel got their bedtime story, and his nibs got his oats (again). The latter is a turn of phrase I hate, but the one he always used.

Realising that sex on a regular basis kept him very sweet-tempered left me feeling like a whore, but I couldn't quite work out what else to do at the present time, since a bear with a sore head I could do without (hate the word whore, but can't help it coming to mind occasionally).

Another row to interrupt my thoughts. Why does everyone in the house want Weetabix when there is only one left, and a whole box of bloody cornflakes they won't look at? Only one way to stop that, I'll have it myself (if I can put up with the squeals).

'Letter for you, Mum,' called Valerie, hanging around waiting for me to open it.

Took it casually, put it on top of television until they had all tripped off to school (glad he's gone to work).

Opened it nervously with fingers on both hands

crossed. A second interview. 'Yippee!' Crikey, that afternoon! Wonder will Jane have the two little ones again? It would be for a while longer this time as I had to stay and listen to the caller. My stomach was turning over. I was pleased but a little apprehensive.

God, it was hot in that hall, I hadn't realised how many women played bingo in the afternoons. Wonder how many husbands know, and how many object?

I watched them milling around, standing in long queues to buy their tickets, overheard their conversations:

'Ooh, there's Mrs So-and-so, she's won three times in a row. Wonder if she'll win today? Don't begrudge her, mind, her old man's been on the sick for years. Nothing wrong with him either, except for a bone complaint – bone bloody idle, ha ha ha.'

Every woman I overheard had some complaint about a man. If only we knew how much we have in common, I thought, we would start a female revolution.

Oh here we go, everyone rushing to their seats, pens out, glasses on, fags lit, and off we jolly well go.

I tried not to be distracted by the concentration on all those faces as I listened hard to the caller.

'And for your first number, on the blue card for one line only, all the sixes, clickety click; top of the house, one hundred; Kelly's eye, number one.' It went on and on, and suddenly I began to feel cold.

'Legs eleven, eighty-eight, two fat ladies, seven-and-six, was she worth it?'

When we got to 'Sweet sixteen', followed by loud wolf whistles from what seemed to be everyone in the hall, I stood up and very discreetly left, the realisation grimly dawning on me.

'It's bloody sexist,' I said out loud once outside the building. Bingo bloody sexist? I can't believe it, it's bloody everywhere.

I wondered if Jane knew what it would be like, and was almost in tears by the time I reached her house.

She had seen me coming up the road and opened the door before I had the chance to knock.

'Was it that bad, love?' she asked.

'I only ever went once,' she continued, 'but I didn't want to dishearten you, thought it better you found out for yourself.'

I couldn't even cry, and my God I wanted to.

'Nothing is funny any more, Jane, the adverts on television, the programmes, I used to laugh like hell at The Two Ronnies, and Benny Hill, but now I feel like putting my foot through the television and breaking a bottle over *his* head, since he still laughs like a drain. What am I going to do, what about my girls. I bet even at their tender ages they're thought of already as sex objects.' That awful feeling of desperation had come over me again, and this morning I had been so happy at the prospect of a job. Now, if my line snapped this afternoon, I'd definitely hang myself.

Jane spoke. 'Look, love, sexism was here before you were born, it will be here when you die, all we can hope to do is make things a little bit better for ourselves in order to make them a lot better for our children, who in turn, if we provide them with enough information, will make it that much better again for their children. That's all we can hope to achieve. It may seem like a piss in the ocean, but it's better than not pissing at all.'

Jane was good at speeches. She was right, too; what the hell would I achieve if I slung in the towel now? My girls might never get to hear from anyone else, so I owed it to them at least.

'It's so hard to point out sexist behaviour on television, or anywhere else, when he sits there grinning from arse to earhole, and actually contradicts me in front of them. It usually starts a row, and the children think that I'm the cause of it all. I can see the girls thinking, "Oh no here she goes again," when I tell them in the middle of some programme that there isn't any need for a particular half-clad woman to be draped over a car to make a sale. They're so confused, their eyes stray from my mouth to his face for confirmation that I'm wrong. I still feel as though I'm fighting a losing battle.'

'You're not. Any point you make will filter through. Make them clear, and without getting in a knot, and it will hit home to at least one of them. Better one convert than none at all,' she laughed.

'Even the books they bring home from school' (I mimed tearing my hair out) 'portray the men digging in the garden, or sitting in their favourite armchair reading a paper, while the women are in the kitchen wearing a pinny.'

'When's your next interview?' Jane laughed.

'I don't know, but give me the benefit of your experience next time, please,' I begged. 'I'd better go.'

74

Jane kissed my cheek, 'I'll keep thinking for you, the right job will come up, you'll see.'

Thomas' little hand tightened around mine. It made me conscious of how careful I should be with him around, he could get quite a complex about his sex, the way he hears me talk about his father. I looked down at his small form. It's an ironing board you'll be getting this Christmas, and your sisters a Meccano set.

I wondered what *he* would have to say about that.

Glad I hadn't told him about my interview. How could I possibly make him understand why I had walked out?

Five

I had hardly got through the front door when the telephone rang. It was his Mum and Dad, I had completely forgotten about their visit, and they had phoned to say that they would be arriving within the hour. I told them how pleased I would be to see them, then sank into a chair looking at the disorder around me. There wasn't time to moan. I had under an hour to clean right through the house and make up a bed in the spare-cum-junk room. Rosie hadn't stirred, so into her cot she went, complete with coat; toys on the floor of the girls' room for Thomas, plus threats of 'If you wake Rosie, I'll kill you.'

I'd never worked so fast before. Everything was literally shoved out of sight. Cupboards bulged; as long as it looked tidy when they arrived, I didn't care about the chaos later, trying to find things. Sheets quickly aired, bed made up – most of the junk in that room was pushed as far under the bed as possible. Kitchen floor mopped and left to dry. Dash into bathroom, soap scraped from basin and bottom of bath, tell-tale ring around bath wiped clean, can actually see in mirror, dead potted plant removed, loo paper off floor and in holder, half bottle of Domestos down pan, shower curtain changed (mildew at the bottom), towels (more like floorcloths) changed, bathmat shaken, floor around it wiped; final touch, fresh-air spray. Window opened, door closed, and left. Breathe sigh of relief.

Our bedroom next. Creep around (please don't wake up, Rosie). Ironing pile, nearly reaching ceiling, shoved into wardrobe, his chair covered with clothes I proceed to fold up (vowed I wouldn't) and put away; found four pairs underpants inches away from washing basket, and five odd socks – he must have eaten the others, can't find them anywhere (clatty swine). Kick empty suitcases (never go anywhere) further under bed, shoes further under wardrobe, look around mildly satisfied, puff up pillows, and throw over covers; dust over dressing table, sling everything in sight in drawers, leaving out talc and deodorant. One shoe lace and an odd slipper (spent a day last week looking for these buggers; must remember) in underwear drawer. Didn't dust window-sill, will close curtains later, won't show.

Must remember to wipe out fridge, stinks of Tuesday's fish (should have defrosted it, can't get to ice box, never mind). Must fix spout on teapot (present from them last year). Must get out lace table cloth (another present, most impractical with children, but it will please her). Good God, haven't enough plates, must ring Jane to bale me out (feel worn out, can't stop now). Three five, half an hour, they will arrive, then children, I'll drop dead. Get pie out of freezer, peel potatoes and carrots, put peas in pot. His father doesn't eat veg – 'Oh but he does love to see colour on his plate,' she always whispers (cantankerous pig).

Thomas shouts to tell me that Rosie is awake, but gets to me first, tugging at jumper. Too tired to have a fight with him, this has got to stop, could feed two calves with this lot. Tempted to read yesterday's paper over their heads but cuddled them both instead.

Pulled down jumper just as doorbell rang, caught sight of myself in hall mirror again, must do something about my hair, beginning to look and feel like candy floss.

'Hello, Mum, how are you? Come in, bet you could do with a cuppa?'

'Could do with using the toilet, dear,' she replied, struggling past me with the suitcase. 'You know what he's like,' she winked. 'Won't stop anywhere for me to go, crossing my legs for half an hour, what with my bladder being weak, and my other trouble.'

'Let me take the case,' I offered, and, looking out of the door asked, 'where is he, anyway?'

'Just parking the car,' she shouted from halfway up the stairs. 'Last time we were here, someone cracked one of the back lights, so he's going to park it in the car park.'

God, we will never hear the last of that, I thought. Probably one of the children in the street. What the hell has she got in this case?

Thomas was immediately at her ankles with a picture book.

'Let your gran get her breath, and say hello to

Rosie,' she said, 'then we will read your book.'

'I'll make you a cuppa now.' Put pan on, still no kettle. 'Then we can catch up on any news.'

Oh Lord, here he comes. 'Hello, Father, how are you?'

'Terrible journey,' he grouched. 'We always seem to meet the maniacs on the road, I think they must lie in wait for us.'

(Bet they think the same, I thought.)

'Near miss on the motorway, wasn't it Gertie?'

'I've told you dear,' she replied softly, 'you aren't supposed to do U-turns, especially in the fast lane.'

'Damn silly woman, I'd have missed the sliproad – added half an hour to our journey that would have, not to mention the extra petrol.'

'Come on, you two, let's have a cuppa,' I intervened (but added in my head, 'Damn belligerent pig').

I watched my mother-in-law with the children. She was so gentle, it was clear how much they loved her. If it wasn't for him, she would be a regular visitor in my house.

'Grandma!' Peace shattered, here's the tribe.

It was obvious who they loved best, too, but a little sad, the way he had to entice them over to him with a 10p piece each for crisps, patting them on the head in a patronising manner. Made my skin crawl.

Everything was organised and dinner was about to be served, when *he* walked in. Valerie had gone discreetly to Jane's to borrow a few plates. The pie looked good, shan't tell him it was a frozen one. Never eats that sort of muck, often heard to say.

A box was pushed in front of me, he winked.

'I'll put a plug on it later, stand it on the draining board.'

A kettle at last. Couldn't have come at a better time; before her stay was over, she would have insisted on buying one. Glad he had been thoughtful for a change.

Children were on their best behaviour, no one whined about the meal, plates were almost licked clean, no one banished from the table, and nothing ended up on the floor, except for a few forgiven crumbs at Thomas' feet.

'That was a good pie,' the old bugger said, burping loudly, pushing himself away from table and spitting in the sink (I could kick him). Cover Thomas' eyes, don't want him to think this is the correct thing to do after a meal.

'Your pastry is a great improvement on the last time.'

I smiled sweetly. If only you knew, craphead.

Mother-in-law bustled around clearing the table, while I ran a bath for Thomas and Rosie.

'Shall we do the dishes for these women?' father-in-law descended to ask (benevolent bastard).

'Well that's nice of you, Harry,' Mother humbled herself. 'Come on, dear, we can bathe the little ones while the men do this.' She sounded excited, couldn't wait to make a mess with them in my nice clean bathroom.

'Where's my glasses, Gertie?' came a shout up the stairs.

'Oh dear, where did he put them?' What a flap she was getting into. 'When did you last have them, dear?' I couldn't believe my ears.

'Do you ever wear them, Mother?' I asked, trying to keep my face straight.

'No dear, of course not,' was her reply.

'Then, why are *you* looking for them?'

'He wouldn't know where to look, dear,' she answered, looking slightly bewildered at my question. The poor old soul didn't know what I was getting at.

It took her a while, but she found them eventually, in the top pocket of his jacket. He was wearing it at the time. She dropped everything to look for those sodding glasses at least three times a day during her visit. I really had to battle with myself not to trample them into the ground (while he was wearing them).

The babies were tucked up in bed (had to feed Rosie in bedroom – it disgusts him). Gertie read bedtime story to enthralled Thomas, Rosie sucked her thumb, almost appearing to be listening.

The girls had a story too, and fell asleep with the most contented look on their little faces that I'd seen in a long while.

Gertie was so easy to love, how could she possibly have ended up with such a pig?

'Just a matter of clearing this littered room, mainly toys, then I'm going to put my feet up for the rest of the evening,' I informed my mother-in-law, 'or what's left of it,' I corrected myself.

'Us men are off to the pub,' father-in-law announced, 'leave you two women to catch up with the latest gossip,' he sneered.

'Funny how women always gossip and men have conversations, isn't it?' I remarked to Gertie when they had left, with no response from her. It all seemed to go over her head.

'Harry's getting more and more short-tempered,' she confessed to me later on, at the same time sewing up a little hole in his jacket pocket. 'My car keys keep falling through, Gertie,' he had bellowed, throwing it at her as he went through the front door, and adding, 'There's a lot of little things like that, that get neglected lately.'

'I'm quite dreading his retirement,' she glanced my way to see my reaction. 'It's not that I'm being disloyal dear, but I've not been feeling quite myself lately. Oh I suppose he's right in a way, I have been putting off little jobs.'

'But if you're not well,' I butted in, 'surely he can give you a hand!'

'He is working all day, dear,' she was quick to defend him. 'I can't expect him to do women's work after a hard day out.'

Gertie began work on a pair of Harry's trousers. She was serious. It made me want to throw up. She looked so frail sitting there, and I thought of the years in front of me with a replica of her useless man (groan, groan).

'I'm thinking of getting a job,' I said after a few minutes silence. The needle relaxed in her hand.

'Don't you think you have enough on your plate, dear?' she asked, diffidently. 'I may be a little old fashioned, but a woman's place is in the home.' She hesitated. 'I know things are done a bit differently these days, but you have got five children and a man to look after. If you had a day's work to contend with on top of that, you would make yourself really ill in no time at all.' She smiled, a warm generous smile. 'I know you may feel a little tied down at the moment, but when the children are grown up and married themselves, you will be able to have a life of your own, get yourself a few hobbies to fill your time,' she laughed, 'between the visits of your grand-children.'

'I need a life of my own now, Mother,' I spoke quietly and with marked precision. 'I feel as though I need something to live for other than housework and children.'

She quoted the old cliché, that must have been handed down to generations of girl children:

'Women are here for one reason dear, as home-makers and mothers. We make our beds and we must lie on them.'

'I have decided to get a job, I made my mind up a while ago. It's just a matter of getting work that will suit me.'

'Have you spoken to you-know-who about it?' She used her son's name as seldom as I.

'No.' I sighed. 'I'm going to get the job, and then tell him.'

'Oh dear, I really don't want to interfere, dear, but do you think that's wise? He's just like his father you know, and Harry would never give his blessing for me to work.'

'I won't need his blessing, Mother,' I said firmly. 'I'll just need him to pull his weight around the house.'

I ignored her bewildered response: 'Do half of your work?'

I was confident by now that half the house was his, half of the children were his, and three quarters of the muck didn't belong to me, and that if under those circumstances I was prepared to wade in, and I found work outside, wade in he would have to as well.

What I wasn't prepared to do was make an issue out of it with a woman I dearly loved, who had no similar understanding because of years of cruel and blatant social conditioning.

She finished stitching up the trousers, folding them neatly in their existing creases, patting them and saying, 'I feel so exhausted, I'll press them in the morning. He does like a nice crease in his trousers.'

And I'd like to put a nice crease straight down the centre of his head, with an axe, I thought.

'Is there anything I can get you, love?' I asked, concerned at her paleness.

'Would you mind very much if I went to bed, dear?' she asked.

'Not at all, I could do with an early night myself.'

'Oh dear, what about supper for the men when they come in? If we both go to bed, they may get annoyed.'

She began to get agitated at the very thought, so to please her I said I would leave them some sandwiches.

Slapped a loaf and a lump of cheese on table in anger, laid bread knife on top and butter at the side of it. Wonder if they will be able to cut bread, I thought, without amputating a thumb or hand.

I followed the weary little form up the stairs.

'It's not very warm in here, Mother, I didn't put the heating on until this morning. I'll get you a hot water bottle.'

'Don't go to any trouble dear, you have enough to

do without fussing over me.'

I put my hand over her lips.

'It's no bother, and what's more a cup of Horlicks in bed will do you good.'

'Yes, Mummy,' she mocked, and laughed.

I had just poured the milk in Gertie's Horlicks, when the front door was closed behind the two excuses for men. My heart sank at the thought of being bullied by the two of them into making their bloody supper.

'Gertie,' mouth almighty shouted, 'I've brought you a bottle of milk stout. Where is she?' he asked, when he hadn't had his usual reply of 'Yes dear, thank you, dear.'

'I'm taking her up a mug of Horlicks,' I said, holding it aloft for his approval.

'Stout will do her more good than that,' he slurred, almost knocking the mug from my hand.

'Come on down here, Gertie,' he yelled up the stairs, waking Rosie, much to my frustration and anger.

She came down like a lamb to the slaughter, her eyes heavy with fatigue. 'If I hadn't, dear,' she explained to me later, 'he would keep on until the whole of the household was awake. Sorry about Rosie, dear.'

'Get this down you, woman,' handing her the bottle, but no glass or cup, 'it will put hairs on your chest,' followed by his hideous raucous laugh.

I stayed in the kitchen, settling and feeding Rosie, while I listened to him going on and on like a stuck gramophone record, with no one else getting a word in edgeways.

He infuriated me when sober, but disgusted me when drunk.

He eventually let her go to bed, but only when he felt tired. Much later on, I guessed when he was asleep, I heard her vomiting in the bathroom. I ran in to her.

'You're not well at all,' I accused. 'Why didn't you tell me?'

'I'm all right dear, I don't like making a fuss. It's just that I can't keep a lot down lately, don't say anything to the men.'

'I won't, but only if you promise me that when you go home you will have a thorough check-up.'

She agreed, and dragged herself back to bed.

She didn't have a check-up as she promised. He had bought her a tonic to 'buck you up, woman' instead. When she finally went to her doctor it was too late. She died two weeks after the visit. The memory of Gertie will be locked up in a special place in my heart until the day that I too take my last breath.

Harry was a broken man at her funeral. I'd never seen a man so bent, crumpled and old, but even as I took his arm to steady him from the steps of the church, my overwhelming pity and grief was for the frail body inside the coffin that had now found peace at so high a price.

He had lost his right and left arm and both his legs in her passing on. She had undoubtedly gained her freedom.

I shared my grief with Jane in the weeks that followed, never once letting the men within an inch of what I thought precious and unique to me. I'd never until that day been particularly religious, but now most nights I would say a prayer for Gertie, me and every women I had ever known.

'Life must and will go on, Gertie,' I said when I was alone one evening. 'I'm going to get that job that I told you about, and work for the both of us. The first year of profits will buy you a headstone fit for a queen, no pauper-looking grave for you.' Under-valued in life, and under-insured in death. The thought made me shudder.

I was feeling lower than I had in months when Jane rang to discuss her latest brainchild with me. The kettle was on and the door open for her within minutes.

She couldn't wipe the grin from her face. 'I've got it, the ideal job. Came to me last night, sitting on the toilet I was, do all my best thinking there,' she laughed. 'I know exactly what this town needs in the present climate of unemployment.' She made a noise like a trumpet. 'Da, da! An employment agency.'

'But we have one,' I responded.

'I'm talking about a private one. There are so many people on the dole at the moment, if we could open a small office, where people could advertise whatever skills they had, and at the same time keep a list of what other people required – home help, painting and decorating . . . Good idea, don't you think? If we did it together, we could split the child care, whenever one works the other has the children. That way I could still manage a small amount of the work I do now.'

'It's a great idea,' I enthused, 'but what would we need in the way of premises and cash?' The very thought of cash brought a dull note into my voice.

'There are quite a few small lock-up shops in town, a few of them unoccupied. Ground floor would be preferable, but not absolutely crucial to start with, as long as we advertise well. It's just a matter of finding out the owners and asking if we can rent. As for cash, simple, a bank loan. Just enough to cover six months' rent, bare necessities in office equipment – desk, chair, typewriter, phone installation, leaving a small sum for a coat of paint and general clear up as needed. That's all there is to it, and what have you got, a jobbing agency!' Jane was really pleased with herself, while I remained slightly nervous about the thought of a bank loan.

'It's a great idea, Jane, I have to hand you that, but the thought of borrowing money, quite honestly God would never agree to it.'

The words had hardly tumbled from my mouth, when she jumped in: 'But it has nothing to do with him, the loan would be in our joint names, with a joint business account.'

I still wasn't sure. 'I've never had an account separate from him. What if he got in touch with the bank manager and put a stop to it? I would feel so embarrassed.'

'Well, I wouldn't have thought that he would go as far as that. But if you're worried we could go to my bank, and simply not tell him.'

I toyed with the thought only seconds. I was dead scared of the damper the man could put on any plans I ever made, but I knew that I had to start somewhere.

I reached for Jane's hand to shake. 'OK,' I said, 'you're on. In for a penny, in for a pound. I'll do it.'

'You won't regret it, let's have a drink on it,' she said, reaching for half a bottle of sherry that had been collecting dust in the corner since Christmas. 'Here's to us, housewives today, hard-headed business women of tomorrow!'

The glass of sherry became three. I could hardly walk straight, and made myself a black coffee as soon as she had gone. I didn't know how long it would take the sherry to reach my breast milk, but I laughed like a drain when I thought about Rosie lying contented and cross-eyed later on that evening.

I wasn't aware of doing the dishes until I was putting the last plate in the cupboard. Ooh I could get into alcoholism easily, I chuckled to myself, falling over the wretched Hoover three times in a row, not even hurting myself, since I was well and truly anaesthetised.

I suppose I ought to make the beds, they haven't been made properly for two days.

'Come on Thomas, upstairs with me while I make the beds.'

'Oh no,' I groaned as I felt in the cots, the two of them were wet. I could have done without this today, I was hours behind on my daily schedule (come to think of it, I hadn't had a schedule for months).

Squeeze myself beside the two cots (must get

Thomas into a bed), didn't look where I was going, foot ended up in potty. God! Disgusting squelch, as poo shoots up leg of trousers, fall flat on my face in desperation to wriggle foot free, cot side slams down to trap hand (choice language, until managed to persuade Thomas to lift cot side gently for swollen hand to be wrenched out).

Don't know what to cry about first, crushed fingers or shit halfway up leg (potty still attached to foot).

Oh God, feel about as happy as a dead cat.

Cleaned up and sobered up by 3.30, thank goodness. Girls have seen him drunk, wouldn't do for them to see Mum falling about uncontrollably too.

Bought a reduced packet of mince in supermarket, smells worse than usual, need four Oxos instead of two. What can I do to cheer it up a bit? Looks terrible colour. Sling in an onion, and half a dead-looking red pepper. Bit better, quick stir and taste: Ugh!

Dinner didn't go down too well, children just ate potatoes and carrots. He quite liked it, thank God, said it was 'different'. Don't quite think it was a compliment, but as near as damn-it from him. Didn't eat mine, *yuk*, revolting.

Scraping waste into bin noticed packet mince had been wrapped in. Good grief! Nearly passed out, had to sit down. I'd given them minced morsels for dogs, clearly printed on side 'not fit for human consumption'. Oh Lord, don't know whether to slash my wrists or give out large doses of syrup of figs. Didn't do either, kept mouth shut, fingers crossed, and eye on toilet door, monitoring visits.

Evening passed uneventfully. Can stop sweating now, danger over, breathe sigh of relief that Rosie wasn't in any danger. No wonder it was cheap.

Called for Jane to ask about any nasty side effects, laughed till she wet herself. 'Let's hope beer doesn't aggravate it,' was her parting shot.

If he's in a good mood tonight, I'll tell him about the agency, I thought as I fished Thomas' underpants from the toilet with a coathanger.

Hazel lost a tooth in school today, found it in her dinner, insisted on me putting it back in her mouth, fixing it to the others with Sellotape. Told her it wouldn't work. Pinched me, the little fiend, when the Sellotape got soggy and it fell out to be promptly swallowed by mangy cat (his cat, male).

'No, I will not go through the cat's poo until I find it.' Poor little mite, gone to bed with swollen eyes. Tried to comfort her, must remember to leave 10p under her pillow.

Chose the wrong time to tell mouth almighty about agency, glad I hadn't mentioned bank loan would be half in my name. I felt very angry with the unsupportive swine. He had laughed, and announced that: 'Women are no good in business, you'll both last a fortnight, no longer. And what about your housework, how are you going to fit that in?'

(Deep breath, wait for it) 'I assumed that if I was bringing in a wage as well as you we would split the work.'

He went grey, his eyes glazed over, and the veins stood right out in his neck.

'WHAT? WHAT did you say? Did I hear you right?

Come home after a day's work and do your work, bloody women's work? You can get that thought right out of your head, I'd be bloody laughed at. You're not on, do you hear me, you can think again, woman.'

I'd never seen him so angry. If I had been sensible, I'd have left further discussion for another time. But I wasn't. I thought the showdown might as well be now.

'You're going to have to pull your weight,' I yelled. 'I've done everything in this house from the start of our marriage! It's too one-sided. I need to work if I don't want to become a bloody vegetable!'

I was stopped mid-sentence. I didn't see the blow coming, but felt the tears spring into my eyes as his hand landed across my nose. I fell back into the chair, feeling glad that we hadn't been upstairs (even then, my first concern was for the children). It was only then that I felt the warm trickle running towards my lips. I wiped at it with the back of my hand and was shocked to see blood.

He stared at me looking shaken, and began to stutter his apologies, running to get a wet cloth and muttering about a cup of sweet tea. All I could think at first was, well the shit really has hit the fan. But guilt came crashing in almost at once to lend its usual helpful hand, as I thought, God, look what I've made him do.

That was the first time he had ever hit me. He looked very shamefaced when he came back with the flannel, slapping it in my face, very nearly giving me a black eye to go with my bleeding nose. But I daren't take a chance and complain in this position.

'I expect you're satisfied, now you have grounds for divorce,' he said, head in hands.

Of course it ended up with me pacifying *him* about my bleeding face.

I can't win, I can't bloody win, I thought, as I told him everything was all right, and that I was sorry that I had provoked him. (I kicked myself a dozen times in the bathroom later.)

I was more determined than ever that this venture with Jane should be a success, and eager to get it started before things became too settled. I'd rather get it over within one fell swoop than let him think that I had given in completely – which is what I knew he would love to think.

Jane and I spent a whole day walking round the town looking for premises in a suitable location and for small rent. One o'clock, and tired out, we pushed the prams and children into a cafe for something to eat.

Only when we had taken the weight off our feet and sat down to order our food did I glance out of the window at the shop opposite.

'Look at that,' I said, standing up, 'look what it says on that shop window; Closing down sale, two days left,' I was gone in a flash, leaving Jane struggling with two hamburgers, two teas and various cakes for the little ones.

'I see you're closing,' I said to the woman behind the counter. 'Do you own the shop?'

'No,' she pointed her finger at the large furniture shop directly opposite, 'the chap that owns that, owns this as well.'

I said 'Thank you', (I think I did), and ran breathless into the furniture shop.

'Can I speak to the owner?' I asked the first assistant I came to.

'Gone to lunch,' was the sullen reply, not even making eye contact with me.

'When will he be back?'

'Dunno, bout arf an hour I expect.'

'Thank you,' I muttered, and ran back to the cafe, and a surprised Jane.

'We could wait here,' suggested Jane.

'Wouldn't dream of moving,' was my reply, stuffing the cold hamburger into my hungry little mouth.

I felt more anxious in that half hour than I had in the labour suite at the maternity hospital. When the hamburger had gone, I started on my nails.

'What's the time? What's the time?' I kept asking a driven-mad-by-me Jane.

'That's about half an hour,' she said finally. 'Go on, see if he's back.'

My tiny feet went nineteen to the dozen as I crossed the road, took a deep breath outside the shop to compose myself, and then swanned in nonchalantly.

'Is the owner back from lunch?' I asked the same assistant, at which she pointed a red fingernail at a man bending over a box in the middle of the shop.

'That's 'im' she said, rather distastefully I thought. No matter, with knees knocking like cymbals I approached him.

'Could I speak to you for a moment?' I asked in my most polite voice.

He looked up. I almost burst out laughing at his bulbous boozy nose.

'What can I do for you?' he smiled, showing a row of black teeth.

'It's about the shop opposite, actually, the one that is closing down. I believe you own it?'

'Yes, but it's already taken,' he said right away, 'if that was what you wanted.'

I could have burst into tears. My heart sank almost to my boots.

'The thing is,' he said, sensing my disappointment, 'there's a large flat on top, and the man that wants the shop is going to have the flat as well. Sorry love, but it's first come, first served.'

'I'll take your phone number, just in case he changes his mind,' he offered as an afterthought.

I gave Jane's, and made my dismal way over to the cafe, shaking my head at an expectant Jane long before I reached her.

'It's gone,' I told her as I fiddled with the spoon in the sugar bowl.

'Hey, it's not our last hope,' she reminded me, 'it could take months to find the right place, we're not going anywhere are we? We just have to be patient, small shops are coming up for rent all the time, we'll get just the thing we are looking for eventually.'

Trouble is with me, I thought, is that I want things to happen the day before tomorrow.

'Come on,' suggested Jane at last, 'we'll go and see my bank manager. At least we could get that part of it sorted out. Might give you a bit of incentive, brighten up our drab lives.'

'Can you come back in about fifteen minutes?' one of the tellers at the bank asked us, 'He has a client with him at the moment.'

'That will be fine,' Jane said, 'enough time for Rosie to drop off to sleep, buy some sweets to keep James and Thomas occupied and stop their tongues wagging while we are trying to talk.'

It was the longest fifteen minutes that I had suffered in quite some time. At last we were heading again in the bank's direction.

The door of an office opened, and a grave looking man called us in, looking at us suspiciously – I thought – over the top of his glasses.

'Good morning, Mr Rawson,' said Jane very confidently.

'And what can I do for you, Mrs Pepper?' he asked, shaking her hand warmly.

'I'd like to arrange a small loan,' she stated, rather than asked, presenting him immediately with all the details of the agency we had planned.

He scratched his chin and fiddled with the end of his pen, but it was obvious from the outset that he was impressed with her frankness.

'It's impossible for me to let you have the deeds of the house as a form of security,' she went on, 'since you know the position between my husband and myself, but I do have a well paid job at the moment, and I wouldn't leave it until the agency showed a good turnover.'

'How much do you think you would need to start yourselves off?' He scratched his chin again and glanced in my direction, which slightly unnerved me.

'I suppose it would depend on what state the

premises was in, and how much we had to spend on repairs and decor,' she told him brightly. 'Then there are telephone connection charges if no phone is there already, plus the bare essentials in office equipment.' She looked thoughtful for a minute or two then said, 'Around £1,500 minimum, as we would also like to cover at least two months' rent, which would dismiss overheads for a while.'

'Why don't you, make it £2,000,' he suggested, 'which would leave a bit spare for any outgoings in the first few months? It could possibly save you having to set up another loan, in case of early difficulties.'

The sum was agreed on, and my heart leapt. I suppose we are half way there, I thought.

'There will be the usual small fee for setting up the loan,' Mr Rawson added, pen poised for us to sign the agreement. 'If we start you off with the minimum repayments each month, we can always review it in six months.'

My hand shook as I put my name to that paper; the first time I'd been taken seriously in the whole of my life. I can't believe it. I'm a joint director of a business! Now all we need is the premises, and the customers. There was a strange gurgle in the pit of my stomach as we walked from that office.

'Not all bank managers are sexist,' laughed Jane. 'That man has always taken me seriously as a person first, then a woman. Well,' she grinned, 'we now have the capital, let's put all our energy into getting the right place, no second best. Right spot, and right price.'

I knew now that nothing short of a holocaust could stop us achieving our goal.

Six

I was walking on air. I didn't even throw a fit when Valerie came home from school with a bottle of Prioderm in her school bag and a note from the nurse to say she had nits. I was bloody annoyed at the insensitive way it was done though, and decided to see her teacher about it, to make sure it was handled with more care for the next child with head lice.

Took all evening to delouse everyone (he wasn't very happy, but slopped it on his head regardless). Had to reassure Valerie that it wasn't her fault, and that she wasn't the dirty little girl she had been made to feel. Decided that evening to tell her about worms too, another supposedly social offence (always kept a packet of Pripsen, just in case).

My highlight of the month; yippee, Thomas has lost all interest in breast milk. Some small hope for my body at last.

Must accept Jane's invitation to go to the gym. Always had a notion that gyms were for the middle classes, not for the likes of me.

'You'll need daps,' said Jane, 'and a tracksuit bottom – something you can bend in, shorts would be ideal.'

'You'll never get me in shorts, what with my varicose veins. I'll wear that velour tracksuit that you gave me, I haven't got any daps though.'

'You can borrow these,' she tossed them at me. 'They will do for the first few times.'

I was as nervous going in the gym as I was going to see the bank manager.

The session cost us £2 each, and my knees knocked as we signed ourselves in (it felt a bit like a Mr-and-Mrs-Smith job, at some sleezy motel).

Changed into exercise gear, and away we went to be drilled by the instructor, a nice, make-yourself-at-home, relaxed woman. We had to check our pulse rate first. Mine was going like the clappers.

'Not unusual on your first visit,' the woman explained. 'As you relax it will become normal.'

I felt such a fool, doing what I thought were school PE things. But by the time I reached the bikes I was raring to go, and thoroughly enjoyed the rest of the session.

'Now for the sauna,' said Jane, stripping off without batting an eye. I wrapped my towel firmly in place, and followed like a Christian to the lions' den.

I peeped casually through the glass in the door while Jane was weighing herself. My God, naked bodies!

'I can't possible go in there,' I hissed at Jane, 'I'll have to get my bra and pants on!' The thought of strangers getting a look at my floppy breasts and varicose veins completely blew my mind.

'You can't do that,' Jane sounded horrified, 'that would be like going to a nudist camp fully clothed.'

Oh God, one, two, three, and in I go. What I hadn't bargained for was seeing Valerie's teacher, how embarrassing, how often do you see, or expect to see, one of your children's teachers in a sauna?

I daren't mention it to Jane, sweated buckets much sooner than her, but was able to leap out of the situation and cool down in the shower. Made a mental note of what day it was in order to avoid the teacher if and when I came again.

Given up smoking for three days. Terribly ratty with the children, but can't see the point of starting to look after outside of my body and neglecting the inside. Been to gym three times. He calls it waste of money and time. Must remember to tell children that when I get desperate for cigarette and behave badly, it's not their fault (also, must tell them without my hands around their throats).

It was two weeks after arranging the bank loan when Jane phoned late one evening. She was completely incoherent on the phone. Decided to pop down to find out what was going on. I met her half way down the street, prancing about like a demented athlete.

'We've got it, we've got it,' she shouted, in a voice loud enough for the next town to hear.

'What, what have we got?'

'The shop, the stop in town. Mr Sutton just phoned, he asked if we were still interested, and said it was ours for first refusal.'

I couldn't stop yelling, and one or two lights went on in the street.

'He's out,' I said, 'come up for a cuppa.'

'I'll just check on the children,' she shouted, as I went on into the house.

We couldn't stop hugging each other, and dancing around the kitchen.

'What happened to the chap that wanted it?' I asked.

'Do you know, I didn't even ask. I was that elated when he offered it, really cheap rent too, £20. Flat included if we want it, ourselves or to sublet. Says it's in a bit of a mess, both places need complete redecoration. I don't know how bad they will be, but we can pick up the keys tomorrow morning and see for ourselves.'

Felt like going out to celebrate, but that could wait until we were ready to open.

'I'm going to have to tell him now,' I groaned, 'what a task.'

Decided, with Jane, that I would tell him it was her business, and that she had offered me a job. Once he could see that it made some money, I would slowly introduce him to the fact that it was half mine. Anything for a quiet life.

The girls were pleasantly surprised at my early start the next morning. Nothing was too much trouble, and I actually sat down and made Valerie's packed lunch in between feeding Rosie.

'Here's 10p each for crisps,' (last of the big spenders) 'and hold Hazel's hand crossing the road, don't run off and leave her.'

Confused look, from Val, as she shouts, 'Won the

pools, Mum?'

'Want some breakfast, love?' and 'You're late this morning,' to him, ignoring his socks on the table.

'Mm, wouldn't mind. I'm out on site this morning, haven't got to be there until ten,' answering both questions at once.

Stuck some eggs in pan, bread under grill, took deep breath and began.

'Jane's starting a business.' My voice was casual. 'She has asked me to give her a hand a couple of days a week.'

'Oh, what sort of business?' he asked.

'An agency, sort of job agency, don't know a lot about it yet. She's getting the keys to a shop this morning, thought I'd go with her, you know, bit of moral support.'

'Don't get too involved, mind,' he warned (little do you know, blabberlips, I thought).

'I'll give her all the help I can, dear, she is a good friend, and I know she would do the same for me.'

'Just as long as you don't whine to me about being tired, and not being able to cope with the kids, if that starts' (the hog) 'you'll stop.'

I chose to ignore his last remark and said, 'Toast is ready, dear,' instead.

Jane knocked minutes after he left the house.

'Perfect timing,' I told her, while I put on my coat. Had trouble with Thomas – as fast as I did up his zip, he would undo it – and resorted to bribery. Very mention of sweets and out of the door in seconds, eyes sparkling and grin from ear to ear.

Everyone we passed within the first five minutes was smoking.

'Could eat one, Jane,' I admitted, but didn't give in.

Badly in need of decoration was an understatement. It was awful. After we had recovered from the initial shock, we made notes of the various repairs. Some we knew that we could do ourselves, but things like plastering we swallowed hard at.

'Let's try the flat,' suggested Jane bravely, feeling for a light switch on the stairs.

That wasn't half as bad as we had expected, judging by the state of the shop.

'I'm sure there must be at least six layers of wallpaper on each wall, and what a hideous colour scheme!'

I agreed. 'But since there won't be any rush to do it, we can concentrate on the shop.'

'I might ask him if he wants to do some plastering,' I added, 'it's a way of getting his approval, I suppose. Do you think it's worth a try?'

'I should say it is, better to have him with us than against us.'

I looked for Thomas and James.

'Did they follow us?' I asked Jane.

'Yes, they were here a minute ago.' She look puzzled.

We walked through the flat calling them, to no avail.

'There's only one room that we haven't tried,' Jane sighed, 'you know what they're like with water.'

'Oh no, the bathroom!' We both made a dive for it.

'The door's locked.' My heart missed a few beats.

'There's water running, too.'

We both pushed our shoulders to the door, it didn't budge.

'Don't panic,' I could hear myself saying, not knowing whether I wanted to reassure Jane or myself.

I looked around blindly for something to hit the door with. 'We will have to talk to them, Jane. I'm blowed if I'm going for Mr Sutton. He might change his mind about renting it to us.'

'Thomas,' I yelled, 'are you having a good time in there?' We both knew that any signs of anger or anxiety would make them as panicky as we were, so we kept as cool as we could.

'Mummy smack Thomas,' we heard a little voice whimper.

'No, darling' (you bloody little swine face) I answered in a flash, 'Mummy wants to play with water too, and Auntie Jane.'

Jane put her hand over her mouth. I knew that the obscenities in my mind were going through hers too.

'Jane's got a duck to float in the water,' she yelled ('or a brick to beat you with,' she whispered to me).

'God, I hope this works.'

Shortly we could hear a pair of feet pattering over towards the door. I set my hands in a strangling position and gritted my teeth, much to Jane's amusement.

The handle of the door started to wiggle about. Jane's hand gripped it, gave it a hefty twist, and it was open.

'My God, I don't think it was even locked,' she sighed, 'just bloody stiff. Well, I'm damn glad we didn't panic and go for help. Imagine how daft we'd have looked, and the remarks that would have been made.' She shuddered at the thought. 'Compose yourself for the mess we'll find inside.'

There was very little mess in fact, but James and Thomas were soaked to the skin. They had found the shower, and among the filth and debris had stood underneath the trickle of water fully clothed.

It was a job to know what to do, clobber them both or thank God they hadn't chosen the bath and drowned themselves.

Relief to find Rosie still fast asleep in pram in the shop where I had left her. Quite forgotten about her actually.

Arranged with Mr Sutton to take over shop that weekend. Very satisfying to be able to pull out a month's rent in advance from back pocket.

Waited until girls came home from school, paid Valerie 50p (business expenses) to keep an eye on Thomas and Rosie, and nipped down to Jane's to make a rough list of things needed in the way of paint etc. Had never plastered in our lives, but determined to do everything ourselves. Bad bits I would ask his master's voice to do.

Stayed longer than I had intended. He was furious, no dinner ready, worse still, no food in house. Left him with a yelling Rosie, ran hell for leather to supermarket – open till six, life-saver.

Even more furious when I got back. Rosie had peed on his trousers. Made me hopping mad: no attempt to change them, just kept looking down at wet patches and swearing.

'Are we getting fed tonight, or are you leaving it till tomorrow?' he asked sarcastically, when I stopped to feed Rosie.

'Won't be long,' I replied, 'unless you're hungry enough to start it yourself?'

His eyebrows nearly hit his cheeks with the size scowl I received.

'Have you been down that bloody shop with her all day?' he pointed in a westerly direction (Jane was always HER when he was annoyed with me).

'As a matter of fact, I have,' I answered, keeping my voice calm so as not to upset Rosie.

'So this is it started, is it? The independent working woman? Is this what I'm expected to put up with every night from now on?'

'If you're that hungry, get a tin of soup, until I've finished feeding Rosie.' I was confused again at this point. Was it a lot to ask, for him to help prepare the meal now and then? Oh, I really don't know. Why do I always end up feeling as though I am in the wrong even if I'm not?

I tried to remember what Jane had said about a woman's guilt. I was still trying to get it into perspective as he banged his way through cupboards for a saucepan. Lived in the house as long as I have, still doesn't know where anything is kept. Shows how much contact he's ever had with the kitchen. (Made a rod for your own back, haven't you? I thought.)

Spent two days breaking our backs at the shop, and that was just the preparation work, cleaning and washing down. Girls came straight from school, they loved it. Not sure whether they were a hindrance or help, but at least involving them meant no hassle and moans from that quarter. Tired as I was I rushed home in time to put meal on table, couldn't bear to have him at my throat at a time like this.

Didn't bother to approach him about plastering, made a reasonable job of it ourselves – it was so satisfying to stand there and admire our handiwork (took ages to get plaster from Thomas' hair, little crow).

Jane didn't seem to get as tired as I did, but then she didn't have five children and a husband to contend with. We plodded on regardless, things were really beginning to take shape. Another couple of days, and the furniture would be in: got a really good deal from Mr Sutton, 20 per cent off desk, very impressed with shop and us.

'Can't wait for the weekend, must have a rest,' I told Jane.

'I think we deserve one,' she admitted, 'you look a bit pale. It can't be good for you to be in this paint-ridden atmosphere. Still breastfeeding, it takes a lot out of you. Make sure you are eating properly.'

She was right, I hadn't been feeling like eating much the last few days. Must be the chemicals we were constantly breathing in.

Terrible evening. Glad to get the girls to bed. Fought and squabbled from the time they came in from school, frightened them all to a complete stand-still when I started to shout, almost lost control, jumped up and down in front of them. Never seen them get their nighties on so quickly.

'That was a bit unnecessary,' he said, once they were in bed.

Typical of him, hides behind paper till it's all over, then bloody criticises.

'Why didn't you stop them, then? Why do you leave it up to me?'

I went upstairs to cry: damned if I will give him the satisfaction of saying, 'I told you so'. I was tired, and wondered if I had bitten off more than I could chew. It's got to get easier, I thought, the hard part is almost over.

Fell asleep on top of the bed for an hour, shocked to find him waking me up with cup of tea in hand. Wonder what he wants, was immediate thought. Didn't take long to find out.

'Father isn't managing as well on his own as I thought he would,' he said quietly. I knew what was coming, but waited for him to speak.

'I'd like to offer him a home with us.' He looked at me for some look of approval. An icy hand gripped my heart.

'We haven't the room,' I answered flatly.

'I've thought of that,' he added in a flash. 'Valerie could double up with Hazel and Wendy, and Father could have her room.'

'No!' My voice was very definite. 'I won't have Valerie pushed in with the others. She's at an age when she needs a certain amount of privacy. Besides I couldn't cope with your father as well, it would be like an extra child, he can't even make a pot of tea.'

'I don't want to argue with you. It's my father, it's been settled already as far as I'm concerned. I've asked him, I spoke to him on the phone today.'

I've never felt so angry. I thought my head would explode.

'You mean, you settled it with him, before even asking my opinion?'

'Yes,' he answered firmly, 'I pay the mortgage for this house. You can like it, or lump it.'

'Then lump it, I bloody well will.'

He left the bedroom, banging the door behind him. Rosie woke, I undressed and took her into bed with me. My breasts were sore as she started to suck and a cold shiver ran through me. My breasts only ever felt sore when I was – oh God, I couldn't even say the word. Oh no, I couldn't be, could I? I had felt sick and tired these last few days.

I sighed heavily. Not another one. I just couldn't stand it. What about the business?

I'm sorry, Jane, I've let you down. Oh dear, she will be so disappointed, still maybe she can find someone else to share it with.

I started to count in my head. The anniversary, two months ago, I'd probably forgotten to take my pill.

Oh God, this is typical of my rotten luck. And now his father is coming to stay. . . I'm much too tired, and upset, to give it any thought tonight.

I feel about as happy as a dead cat.

I was sick as soon as I got out of bed. He gave me an odd look. Ignored it and him.

Sobbed for a full hour with Jane.

'I could cope with the pregnancy,' I spluttered, 'but not his father. Jane, can you imagine what it will be like, to live with the two of them? My girls won't stand a chance, Thomas neither for that matter.'

'You could give him an ultimatum,' she suggested. 'His father or you?'

'What's the betting he would choose his bloody father? Besides, he knows I've got nowhere to go.'

'There's always the flat,' she offered.

'But that was to be an extra income for us. I couldn't pay any rent. I wouldn't have any money – except the family allowance, that's the only thing in my name.'

'It's worth thinking about. He doesn't know you have that card up your sleeve.'

'I'll do it,' I said. Thinking of that little bit of power made me feel a lot happier.

Cooked the evening meal in silence, speaking only when spoken to. Didn't seem to bother him, he could keep silences going indefinitely.

Just about to settle Rosie when Valerie burst into the bedroom.

'Mummy, Daddy has moved my bed in with Wendy and Hazel. I'm not going to sleep in their smelly room, I want my own room back!' she yelled at the top of her voice.

I tried to calm her down. 'Look, darling, has Daddy told you the reason for moving you in with the girls?'

'Yes,' she yelled even louder, 'Grandad is coming to stay. Does he have to MUM?' she pleaded, 'He picks his nose at the tea table, and spits in the fire, and he gets all my homework wrong by interfering with it.'

There was no answer to her moan. I felt as wretched as her; I hadn't seriously thought that the pig would go ahead with it in spite of everything.

'Father is moving in tomorrow,' he said drily, rolling over in bed and snoring like a bull elephant.

Right, I thought, plan of action coming up.

I awoke a little earlier than usual, packed as much into two large suitcases as I could, and hid them out of the way in the cupboard under the stairs.

'You're not going to school today,' I told the girls as they wandered, half asleep, one at a time down the stairs.

'Where are we going?' asked Valerie, quite excited.

'I'll tell you later,' I winked, as I poured the milk on to the cereals.

All five children were bathed and dressed. He wore a look of confusion, but never once asked why they weren't at school.

Harry's car drove up to the house at 10:30.

Putting Rosie into her pram, I gave the order:

'Right, coats on, children!' His face was a picture, but he remained defiantly silent.

One of the cases fitted nicely on top of the pram, the other in my hand, as Harry passed through the hall with his suitcase and we filed out.

'I hope you will both be very happy,' I turned round to say to the two open-mouthed farts, before closing the door behind us.

I didn't want to stop at Jane's in case it would involve her, so made my way straight down to the shop.

Glad to be able to put suitcase down on step; my hand was purple and creased from the weight of it.

The flat wasnt't too bad at all and once I had lit a fire it looked quite cosy in fact.

The girls were off, getting their priorities right by choosing the most comfortable room to sleep in. The furniture was sparse, and not exactly Ritz style, but would do for the time being.

I rang Jane as soon as the two young ones were settled for a morning nap.

'I'll bring some blankets and sleeping bags down right away. I have plenty of spare ones. Stick the kettle on, I'll be down in ten minutes.'

I told her what had happened.

'I wish I had been a fly on the wall, to see the expression on their faces. He must have been dumbstruck,' she giggled. 'How long do you intend to stay?' she asked, looking around at the awful colour scheme.

I stuck out my chin stubbornly, 'As long as is necessary.'

'We could maybe put a lick of paint around the place, it would look a bit more cheerful. Where are your things? I'll help you unpack while the children are occupied with investigating the place.'

She picked up the suitcase, lying in the centre of the room, and pulled a face.

'Good Lord, what have you got in this? You didn't walk down with this, did you?'

'Yes,' I answered, surprised at her remark. 'Why?'

'Well, the baby,' she pointed to my tummy.

I gasped, 'I didn't give it a thought! I should be all right, it wasn't far,' I tried to reassure myself.

'Well, take it easy, have an early night tonight.'

'I think I've sprained my ankle!' Hazel shouted

from the living room.

'I'll sprain your bloody neck if you don't stop jumping on that settee, I've got to sleep on that. The springs will go if you keep using it as a trampoline!'

'You always spoil our fun,' she muttered, just loud enough for me to hear.

I smiled at Jane, 'Happy families, dear.'

The children took a long time to settle that night. I had anticipated that but had more trouble with Wendy than all the others put together. Her nightlight hadn't occurred to me and I ended up hanging over the edge of the narrow settee with her squeezed firmly beside me.

It was about 2.30 that morning when the contractions started. I leapt out of bed, ran to the bathroom, and discovered a large brown stain in my pants. I was horrified. I knew in a split second (as women often do) that I was going to lose this baby. The poor little sod had never had the chance to be loved and wanted even for a moment since its conception, that's the bit that hurt most.

The whole of my body was racked with pain by the time I phoned Jane. 'Please don't let it happen in front of the children,' I prayed.

I phoned an ambulance as soon as I knew that Jane was willing to take over with the children (I hadn't actually doubted it for a minute). The two arrived within minutes of each other, no time to kiss the children goodbye, and no time for the sobs that were churning inside me.

I don't remember getting to the hospital, but I know it must have been jet propelled. The ambulance men were wonderful, no time to thank them.

Within the hour my baby had gone. An incinerator, I hazily supposed. I was left depressed and empty, not able to think even of my five young back at the flat.

I cried all night and into the early hours of the next day. One misguided kindly soul had said, 'Well, you have got five, dear.' I knew something that she didn't, that number six would have been loved and wanted too.

Because of the speed of the miscarriage there was the added fear that I might haemorrhage if I didn't rest well, so the doctor advised me to have hospital supervision for a few days.

Jane was a brick and moved the children in with her until I came home. She brought them in to see me that evening; it looked like a school outing as she filed through the ward with the seven children. Although it was usually against hospital rules for that many visitors to one bed, they thoughtfully turned a blind eye, since they were in no way disruptive.

'You may not like this,' Jane spoke quietly over the children's heads, 'but Valerie went to see her father last night, and told him what had happened.' She waited for my reaction before continuing.

'It's only fair that he should know, however hurt you are about the other situation.'

I knew she was right, and no sooner had she finished speaking than I saw him standing in the doorway of the ward, looking from bed to bed. He smiled brightly when he saw me, and Hazel and Wendy ran up to greet him. Valerie was more concerned about the reprimand that she might get from me, but I smiled, squeezed her hand, and told her how right she had been.

'Flowers and grapes,' I smiled, and didn't pull away as he kissed my cheek.

'I'm sorry, love,' he whispered. 'I had no idea.'

Jane very diplomatically decided to take the children out so that we could talk (even though I felt as though there was nothing to say).

'Don't forget my breast milk,' I waved, holding out four little bottles.

I expected the children to cling to me, weeping. Most disappointing they didn't, seemed quite eager to go in fact.

'Why didn't you tell me you were pregnant?' he asked when Jane left.

'I didn't know myself, until a few days before I left,' I answered. 'You were pretty unapproachable, anyway.'

'Will you come home, when you are discharged from here?' he asked.

'Will Harry be there?'

'He would be able to help with the children, to give you a proper rest. He's very upset, you know,' he hastily added.

'I will not live with you and Harry,' I firmly answered. 'I'll be going back to the flat over the shop.'

'You're being bloody stubborn,' he spat at me, 'you won't be able to manage on your own.' He stood up to go. 'You'll be back with your tail between your legs.' With that generous passing remark, the fathead was gone.

'I won't be back,' I said to the empty chair. Whose

tail between whose legs, I smiled.

The taxi dropped me off outside the shop. I knew Jane would be there, she had phoned to tell me, so the door was open.

What an unbelievable surprise greeted me on walking up the stairs. Jane had put a coat of white paint everywhere, and decorated the kitchen and living room. It was amazing to see the difference, and in so short a space of time. It really looked welcoming.

I was made to sit down, and a cup of tea produced in minutes. I don't remember a time when tea tasted so good. Rosie woke on cue. It was wonderful to hold her and feed her again, and to feel Thomas' clambering little hands all over me. I couldn't wait for the girls to come home from school.

'I thought I'd take them up to the house with me this afternoon,' said Jane, pointing to Thomas and Rosie. 'You could express some milk for her next feed. It would give you the chance to go to bed for a couple of hours and I'll meet your girls from school. I'll give them their tea, so that you won't need to bother cooking.'

Jane laughed when I thanked her.

'There is an ulterior motive, you know. I want you to rest up for the next few days because I thought we could open the agency on Monday. I managed to get an ad in the paper for this week and next, and the press might even think we are worth a write-up. The more publicity we can get, the better it will be for business. Oh, and we already have a chippy, and a brickie on our list.' She sounded pleased with herself.

Just talking about it filled me with renewed excitement and enthusiasm.

I hadn't realised how tired I was until I lay down on the settee. I don't know how long I slept, but if it was any indication, when I woke up the fire had gone out.

A shower was what I needed. Anything to fill time; it was quiet and lonely without the little monsters.

Jane came in around seven. Poor Thomas was dropping on his feet. I didn't even wash his face, just stuck him into his sleeping bag as he was, removing only his coat and shoes. He was asleep as soon as his head touched the pillow.

Rosie fed until her tummy looked fit to burst. Valerie was helpful and sorted the nightdresses out. 'Can we wear cardigans to bed?' she asked. 'We haven't got our hot water bottles.' That was yet another thing I'd forgotten to bring with us.

Once the children were settled, I sat down with Jane to make out a list of various things that I wanted from the house.

Hazel's nightlight, hot water bottles, spare blankets, some crocks, pots and pans, and the coffee table that Gertie had given me.

As I made out the list, I wondered how long I would be here.

I had a hard job making up my mind whether to knock on the door one evening when I knew he would be there, or to use my key during the day and creep in like a thief in the night (well, day). I decided to go during the day. I wanted to avoid a scene at all costs and Harry I could handle.

'I'm going to brave it tomorrow,' I told Jane as she was leaving. She wished me luck, and went on her way.

Let's count heads, I said to myself, checking on the girls, then to bed myself. The girls looked adequately warm and comfortable, huddled together on a mattress in the centre of the bedroom floor. Thomas too seemed happy in his sleeping bag beside them.

Lucky Rosie hasn't yet outgrown her pram, I thought, as I settled down on the lumpy threadbare settee, wondering how long it would be before Wendy's tiny body would be clambering in with me.

The morning routine was slightly altered, since the girls now had a main road to cross for school. They assured me that a lollipop man was on duty to see the schoolchildren across the road, but I needed to see for myself. Meant an extra rush with Thomas and Rosie, Valerie, storming off ahead of us with that 'you don't trust me' look spreading across her face.

Reluctantly I left them to go the rest of the way without me. Only then did Valerie concede to smile at me and wave (little crow).

Walked slowly towards the house. No sign of car, put key in the lock, my heart pounding. Curtains still pulled together in living room, light left on – made me smile, one of his biggest moans was the quarterly electricity bill. State of the kitchen brought me to a standstill; another meal's dishes left, and it would have been virtually impossible to see the sink.

Months before I would have had a surging urge to get stuck into it, but now I only stood back in amazement. Took the only clean saucepan, and half a dozen mugs. Now the swine would have to wash up, I chuckled as I put them in the case.

I heard the door close, thinking it was Harry I didn't even turn around. When I eventually did, I was taken by surprise to see him in the doorway.

'You're back are you?' he smiled, looking at the suitcase. 'You'll find your work's cut out for you,' and he pointed at the sink.

He rendered me bloody speechless! He actually thought I'd come back to clear his debris.

'I just came for a few things that the girls need.' I hoped that my voice didn't sound as shaky as it felt. 'I'd like the coffee table too, that Gertie gave me. It will come in handy for the children. By the way, they send their love.' (That was an afterthought, they hadn't.)

'How long is this nonsense going to go on?' he asked, as I closed the case and got ready to go. I ignored the bombastic remark.

'Thomas is upstairs getting a toy, he'd like to see you. Is the rabbit dead yet? When I can sort things out a bit, I'll come for him.'

His face was a picture. What was the man expecting? Whatever it was, it hadn't materialised with my visit.

He gave Thomas £1 and told him to share it with the girls. He hovered about on the doorstep until we were well out of sight. I couldn't resist the temptation to look over my shoulder, and my heart gave a funny little turn. Pity, guilt, or bloody relief.

The phone was ringing when I got into the shop. It was him.

'Can I pop in tonight, to see the children?'

'Of course you can,' I answered brightly.

The girls were pleased to see him. He played with them for an hour before helping me – voluntarily – to put them to bed.

The least I could do was make him a cup of tea. As we sat drinking it, he cleared his throat as if to make some sort of speech.

'I'd like you to think about coming back,' he spoke at last, 'the house is in a terrible mess, and I can't work out how to use the washing machine. Did you take the book of instructions with you? Father is driving me mad, he can't boil an egg without difficulty, and he will sit by the fire letting it go out, before he'll put a lump of coal on it.' He looked at me. 'The house isn't the same without you.'

I couldn't believe my ears. Not once had he said that he had missed me or the children.

'I shouldn't worry about not being able to use the machine,' I said.

'Does that mean you're coming back?' he asked, quite enthusiastic.

'No,' I replied, 'I'll be having the machine here. It goes with the children, and they're with me. Besides, it's me that has made all the payments up till now.'

When I saw him to the door, I couldn't help thinking tht he looked as happy as a dead cat.